The Happy Hollisters at Snowflake Camp

BY JERRY WEST

Illustrated by Helen S. Hamilton

GARDEN CITY, N.Y.

Garden City Books

Contents

CHAPTER 1

A Television Surprise

"MOTHER, come here quick!"

Ricky Hollister raced through the living room to the foot of the stairway. His freckled face was flushed with excitement and his reddish hair was mussed like most seven-year-old boys'.

"What's the matter?" came a sweet voice from the second floor.

"Gram and Gramp are on television!" Ricky shouted.

"Are you sure?" asked Mrs. Hollister, hurrying down the steps. She was a slender, youthful woman with blond hair and blue eyes, which were now wide with wonder.

"Sure I'm sure!" Ricky said as he took her hand. "Hurry before it's all over!"

The boy pulled his mother toward a corner of the living room, where her four other children were gathered around the television set watching a Saturday-morning program. It was a motion picture of winter sports events in Canada, and at the moment a ski jumper was flying through the air.

5

"He's flapping his arms like a bird's wings!"

"He's flapping his arms like a bird's wings," giggled little Sue, who was four.

"Mother, you're too late," said Holly, a pert-looking six-year-old with brown pigtails. She was lying on the floor, resting on her elbows.

Beside her was dark-haired Sue, sitting crosslegged. She held a curly-headed doll in her lap.

"My baby saw Gram and Gramp, too," said Sue, making her doll's eyes blink.

"We'll probably see them again," spoke up Pam Hollister, a pretty blond girl of ten. She was seated on a hassock beside her brother Pete, a husky lad of twelve with a crew cut.

Pete turned toward his mother. "I'll get a chair for you," he said politely, and dragged one nearer the screen.

Mrs. Hollister sat down to look at the fascinating picture.

"What were Gram and Gramp doing?" she asked.

"They were watching a snowshoe race," Pete explained. "This film was taken at Froston last year during the Trappers' Carnival."

"Look!" Ricky exclaimed. "There they are!"

The faces of the spectators flashed onto the screen again. Among them were Gram and Gramp Hollister. Their faces showed so clearly that Sue hopped up to kiss them.

"Hello, Gram! Hello, Gramp!" she said, holding a pudgy finger against the glass.

"Please sit down, Sue," Ricky pleaded. "I can't see them."

As the little girl dropped to the rug, her mother said, "Isn't this wonderful!"

It almost seemed as if Gram and Gramp had heard her, for they turned to face the family, smiling directly at them. The children clapped gleefully.

The elder Hollisters were young-looking grandparents. But what was more important they looked as if they, too, were happy Hollisters like their relatives in Shoreham.

Gram, dressed in a fur coat, with a scarf over her hair, had a round face and eyes that sparkled with humor. Gramp, in a storm coat and a fur cap, was lean and rugged. He had a straight nose, and the corners of his mouth looked as if he were always about to burst into a big smile.

"Gram and Gramp on TV!"

"Oh, they're breathing out smoke!" Holly said, startled.

"That's only their breath," Ricky said with an air of authority. "It's awful cold at Froston."

"I wish Daddy could see this," Mrs. Hollister said as the scene changed to show a dog-sled event. The announcer's voice told the television audience that this was an unusual race.

"Watch this event closely," he suggested.

"What lovely Eskimo dogs!" Pam said admiringly, as the strong animals pulled the sleds into position.

"They're not as nice as our Zip," Ricky said. "Here, Zip, where are you?" he called.

But their pet collie was outdoors frolicking in the crisp November weather. The boy thought he might be chasing rabbits in the woods.

"Well, Zip is the best dog in Shoreham," Pete agreed. "But crickets, aren't those Huskies great!"

"Now they're lining up for the race to start," Mrs. Hollister said, by this time as excited as her children.

"There they go!" Pam cried out. "See them pull!"

Straining at their harnesses, the dogs raced along, their plumed tails blowing in the wind. There were five teams in the race. Each sled was pulled by four dogs, one behind the other. There was one passenger, and a driver who stood in the rear. The crowds cheered first for one team, then another.

"What are we s'posed to watch for, Mommy?" Sue asked when the teams were halfway around the race course.

"I don't know, dear," came the reply. "But look carefully. Perhaps there will be a surprise."

As the dogs headed for the finish line, the Hollister children jumped up and down with excitement. One team, led by a beautiful big Husky, was in the lead and rapidly pulling away from the others.

Suddenly the announcer's voice said, "The lead dog of this team is named Fluff. It looks as if her sled will be the winner."

The children hitched closer to the television screen so they would not miss a single detail.

Suddenly Pam cried out, "Oh dear! Something's happened!" and her brothers and sisters groaned.

Fluff had stumbled and fallen head over heels in the snow!

The other dogs in the team piled up behind her, and the sled veered off the course.

"Poor Fluff is hurt!" Holly cried.

"The second sled is gaining!" Pete said in despair.

"Come on, Fluff, get up and win!" Pam urged.

But the lovely dog lay in the snow, while the second team raced across the finish line, the winner.

"That's too bad," Mrs. Hollister told her disappointed children as the program ended and Pete turned the set off.

"Yikes!" Ricky scrambled to his feet. "What made Fluff fall down?"

"I wish the announcer had told us," Pam said with a downcast look. "The poor dog!"

"Since that movie was taken a year ago," Mrs. Hollister said, trying to cheer them up, "Fluff probably is all right by this time and racing again."

The lovely dog lay in the snow.

"I hope so," Pam said with a sigh.

She loved animals, especially Zip. Pam's gentle brown eyes suddenly brightened as she heard the frisky collie scratching at the kitchen door.

Pete let him in. Zip trotted into the living room smelling like the fresh outdoors and autumn leaves. Pam hugged him and said:

"We saw Gram and Gramp on television. Do you remember them?"

Zip gave two short barks, as if to answer yes, then settled down at the girl's feet.

"Won't Gramp and Gram be thrilled that we saw the Trappers' Carnival?" Pam remarked. "I wish we could see them more often."

Gramp and Gram, parents of Mr. Hollister, had moved to Canada after Gramp had retired from business in the United States. Now they operated a group of cabins known as Snowflake Camp. The place was very popular with winter vacationists, and Gram and Gramp enjoyed running it.

"And I wish I could go to see a Trappers' Carnival," Pete sighed.

"Perhaps we shall," Mrs. Hollister said, rising and walking toward the kitchen. "Who would like to set the table while I prepare lunch? Daddy will be home from the store any minute."

"I will," said Pam and Holly together.

The older girl spread a checkered cloth on the dining-room table while her sister went to get the dishes. Their father usually came home at lunch time from *The Trading Post*. Mr. Hollister had bought the hardware business the previous spring, so the family had moved to Shoreham. He had added toys and sporting goods, and the store soon became popular with people of all ages.

"Here comes Dad now!" Ricky called out.

A station wagon was rolling into the driveway. It stopped in front of the garage, and a tall, good-looking man stepped out. Ricky opened the door for him and took his coat to hang in the closet.

After Mr. Hollister had kissed his wife, the children flocked about him. They all talked at once, creating a good bit of confusion.

"Daddy, we saw Gram and Gramp on television!"

"May I have skis like the men in Froston?"

"And shoe snows for me," cried Sue, who often mixed up her words.

"Poor Fluff lost the race!"

"When may we go to Froston?"

Mr. Hollister grinned. "Wait a minute!" he cried. "What's this all about—Gram and Gramp on television. Is that right, Elaine?"

"It's true, John," his wife replied. "I wish you had seen it."

The children told him about the show.

"They're television stars," Holly said proudly. "Just like Fluff."

"Fluff? What's Fluff? Sounds like a powder puff to me," her father said, his brown eyes twinkling.

"When may we go to Froston?"

Holly giggled, then answered, "Fluff is a Husky dog who lost the race because she fell down."

At this moment Mrs. Hollister rang a tinkling bell. To the children, the bell always seemed to say, "It's mealtime!"

When they were seated and had been served, talk once more centered around Froston and the Trappers' Carnival.

"It would be so nice to visit Gram and Gramp for the carnival this year," Pam said dreamily.

"Will it be given soon, Dad?" Pete asked.

Mr. Hollister explained that the Trappers' Carnival was held each year on the week end after Thanksgiving. In this way, the event attracted many visitors from the United States.

"It marks the time when the trappers set off into the woods," he explained. "They go for the wild animals whose skins are used to keep people warm."

"You mean like Mommy's fur coat?" Sue asked.

"That's right," her father replied. "And up where the Huskies come from people wear fur a good part of the year."

Suddenly Ricky said, "Dad, you've been to Gram and Gramp's place. What's it like?"

"Pretty exciting, son. In the winter the snow is very deep. Sometimes the drifts get as high as the cabins and you have to shovel your way out. It's hard for the mailman to get around."

"Does he use reindeer like Santa Claus?" Sue asked.

"No. He uses a snowmobile. That's a car with skis on the front."

"Oh, I want to see it!" Holly cried.

"And ride in it," Pete added.

"Are there lots of wild animals up there, Dad?" Ricky asked.

"Oh yes. Deer, bears, wolves. The bears sleep all winter of course, but the others are around."

Pete asked if there were any Huskies and was told that none ran wild around Snowflake Camp.

"I've heard that a few people have them for pets, though," Mr. Hollister explained.

Suddenly Holly broke into the conversation. "Daddy, it's not long to Thanksgiving. We have several days off from school. Can't we go to the Trappers' Carnival?"

Mr. Hollister smiled. "Not enough time off,

though. Snowflake Camp is a long way from here," he said.

Then, seeing the looks of disappointment on his children's faces, he relented a bit.

"I suppose we might work it somehow," he said. Then he shook his head. "But come to think of it, there's one big drawback."

"What's that?" the children chorused.

"I recently had a letter from Gram," Mr. Hollister said. "Every single cabin has been taken for Thanksgiving week end because of the Trappers' Carnival."

Pam spoke up. "Surely Gram and Gramp wouldn't refuse to let us visit them. Daddy, please may I write and ask them?"

Mr. Hollister smiled. "It won't do any harm to try," he said. "There might be a cancellation."

"Daddy, let's visit Gram and Gramp."

CHAPTER 2

A New Club

WHILE the other children helped their mother clear away luncheon, Pam sat down to write the letter to Froston.

By the time the dishes were washed and the kitchen swept, she appeared with a neatly addressed envelope.

"I'll take it to the mailbox," Holly volunteered.

"And I'll help you," Sue offered.

The sisters put on their heavy jackets and hurried down the street to mail the important letter. The trees that lined the sidewalk were nearly bare of leaves now and the grass was brown. But Pine Lake, at the back of the Hollisters' large, old-fashioned house, was as beautiful as in the summertime. The water was clear and the pines which dotted its shoreline wore the same attractive green dress.

As Holly dropped the letter into the box, she said, "I hope, I hope, Mr. Postman with the snowmobile, that you will send us a good answer back."

"Oh yes, please do," Sue added.

When the little girls returned to their big yard they found Ricky standing under the willow tree on the

"It's make-believe snow."

shore front. He was grasping a large paper sack. It seemed to be heavy.

"What's in there, Ricky?" Holly asked, walking over to peek into the bag.

"Snow," the boy replied.

"It isn't snow at all," Holly said, wrinkling her nose. "It's flour."

Ricky grinned. "It's make-believe snow. Look, I'll show you the start of a neat game. Make believe we're in Froston at the Trappers' Carnival."

He began to sprinkle the flour over the ground.

"We're having a snowstorm," he said.

"I'll be the North Wind!" Sue offered. She filled her cheeks with air and blew hard.

"I'm going to make a pair of snowshoes," Ricky said after he had scattered all the flour. "Want to help?"

"Oh yes. What shall we do?" Holly asked.

"Get me a ball of twine, will you?"

Holly ran into the house. She returned with the twine and gave it to her brother.

On the ground about them lay many thin willow branches. Ricky picked up two and twisted them into the shape of snowshoes. He handed one to Holly.

"You string this snowshoe and I'll work on the other," he said.

While Sue looked on, her brother and sister sat down and crisscrossed the twine, looping and tying the ends over the branches. Finally Sue giggled.

"They look like little tennis rackets," she said.

"Wait until after we've played this game," Ricky said.

When the two homemade snowshoes were finished, the boy placed them on the ground side by side. As he tied them onto his feet, he said:

"Now I'll track down the wolves! I'm a trapper!"

"Who's going to be the wolf?" Sue asked.

Just then Holly spied Zip frisking in the weeds near their dock. Just what they needed for the game! She called him and the collie raced to her side.

"You're a wolf," Holly told him as she led the dog through the flour snow. "Ricky's going to track you."

Zip looked up at Holly and gave a little whine as if to say he did not understand the game. But when Holly led him across the flour again, he seemed to get the idea.

"This is the way the woodsmen do it."

"Here I come after you!" Ricky shouted, and he tramped across the flour snow.

Sue and Holly laughed to see their brother waddling like a duck.

"I have to lift my feet high," Ricky explained. "That's the way the woodsmen do it."

Zip entered into the fun and kept out of Ricky's reach for a while before letting the boy catch him.

"It's my turn now," Holly said. "Let me use the snowshoes."

Ricky helped Holly put them on her feet. By this time Zip knew exactly what to do. He circled around in the flour a few times, then trotted off, making little white marks on the grass with his paws. Holly went after him, giggling as she lifted her feet high off the ground.

"Hurray, I caught the bad wolf too!" she cried as Zip rolled over on the ground and let Holly "tag" him.

"I want a turn," said Sue eagerly.

"Of course, honey," her sister replied. "Here, I'll help you."

As Holly tied the snowshoes on Sue's feet, the little girl said, "I don't want to walk over just snow. Put some ice with it, Ricky."

"That's easy," her brother replied, snapping his fingers. "I'll put water on the snow and it'll freeze."

Ricky ran to the lake front and picked up a tin can sometimes used to hold fishing worms. He bent down and scooped some water in it. Then he hurried back to the patch of "snow" and sprinkled the water on the flour.

"There," he said proudly. "Best make-believe ice in Shoreham."

Sue smiled and stepped on the gooey white mass. It clung to the bottom of her snowshoes.

"Oh, dear, this is the stickiest ice I ever saw," she complained, and leaned over to wipe the dough from her feet. But as she did, swish—boom! Sue slipped and sat down hard.

"Now you've done it!" Ricky said. "The 'ice' is all over your dress."

He and Holly helped Sue to her feet. Together, they tried to wipe off the sticky flour, but only succeeded in getting their hands full of it. Finally Holly said:

"You'd better run in the house to get cleaned up. We'll go with you."

When the three children were halfway up the steps, Mrs. Hollister came to the door.

"Goodness!" she exclaimed. "What have you been doing? Don't track that paste into the house, Sue. Wait there until I get a cloth."

Mrs. Hollister disappeared a few moments, then returned with a damp cloth and began to wipe the sticky stuff from Sue's feet and dress. She handed rags to Ricky and Holly and said:

"Please clean the steps, children, and play another kind of game. Why don't you three rake the leaves in the front yard?"

The youngsters liked this idea.

"Let's make a big pile of them and jump in it," Holly suggested.

Ricky hurried into the garage for a couple of fan-shaped rakes and a toy one for Sue. Soon the children were busy raking up the crisp brown, red, and yellow leaves. In a few minutes they had a high stack of them in the middle of the yard.

"Ready for the jumps!" Ricky commanded as he lined up his sisters near the pile.

First Sue ran and leaped into the leaves, squealing with delight. When she arose, they were sticking to her hair and tickling her nose.

Holly had a turn and Ricky followed. He rolled over and over, scattering the pile.

"I have another idea," Holly said. "Suppose I lie down and you cover me up."

When she lay down, Ricky and Sue picked up big armfuls of leaves and dropped them on top of her. Finally Holly could not be seen. As Ricky scooped up more leaves for good measure, Dave Mead, a friend of Pete's, streaked into the yard on his bicycle.

"Hi, where's Pete?" he called as he headed for the pile of leaves. Ricky thought Dave was going to stop, but the boy shouted, "Here I go right through your leaves!"

Ricky and Sue were so frightened that at first they could not make a sound. But finally Ricky shouted:

"Stop, Dave! Holly's under there!"

Dave jammed on his brakes. The back wheel locked, and the bicycle skidded to a stop one inch from Holly's head!

Holly popped out of the leaves.

When she heard the screeching tire, Holly popped up. Not realizing the danger, she said gaily:

"Hello, Dave. If you want Pete, he's in the house."

"Whew!" was all Dave could say, glad he had not hit her.

"Are you fellows going to a football game?" Ricky asked, hoping to be invited to go along.

"No," Dave replied as he propped his bicycle against a tree. "I came to tell you some news."

Just then Pete and Pam came from the house and ran up to the others.

"Guess what!" Dave said. "I hear we're going to have a swell new club at school."

"Really?" Pam asked. "What kind of club?"

"I don't know," Dave replied. "The story's around that Mr. Russell will tell us Monday."

Mr. Russell was the principal of Lincoln School, where the Hollisters had enrolled two months before. The children liked their new teachers, especially Miss Nelson, who had Pam's class. The Hollisters got along well with all their classmates with the exception of Joey Brill, the neighborhood bully. This unpleasant boy was always making trouble for them.

All the children were excited about the new club.

"I can hardly wait till Monday!" Pam exclaimed. "I do hope it's one I can join."

After they had made a dozen guesses about the kind of club it might be, all the children went in the house to watch a football game on television. But the new club was uppermost in their minds.

They hurried to Miss Nelson's room.

When Monday morning came, Pete, Pam, Ricky, and Holly set off for school. When they arrived they found other children talking about the mysterious club. But no one knew what it was.

"We haven't long to wait," Pam said excitedly, as the bell rang for assembly.

After all the students had filed in and sung "The Star Spangled Banner," Principal Russell motioned the children to be seated. He made several announcements before mentioning the new club and everyone was fidgety. But finally he said:

"Miss Nelson is going to form a Pet Club. Anyone may join."

Everybody clapped enthusiastically. When they stopped, Mr. Russell added:

"I'm glad you like the idea. Many children who have pets want to learn more about animals' habits, so this will be a good opportunity to study them. The club will organize in Miss Nelson's room after school today."

The Hollister children could hardly wait for the final bell to ring. When it did, Pete, Ricky, and Holly hurried to join Pam in Miss Nelson's room. By the time the teacher rose to speak, the room was filled. Miss Nelson, a short, dark-haired woman with a friendly smile, counted those present.

"Twenty-five club members!" she exclaimed. "That's splendid." Then she told them that the Pet Club would meet once a week. First they would elect officers and then plan their program.

"I'll be the president!" called a voice from the rear of the room.

The children turned around to see who it was.

"Ugh! Joey Brill!" Ricky whispered, gazing at the tall, heavily built boy of twelve.

"Does anybody nominate Joey?" Miss Nelson asked.

A boy sitting beside Joey did this, grinning. A girl named Alma on his other side seconded the motion.

"Joey must have planned this in advance," Dave told Pete quietly. Dave raised his hand. "I nominate Pam Hollister," he announced. "She loves animals and knows a lot about them."

"I second the motion," said Ann Hunter, Pam's best friend.

"A girl can't be president!" Joey stormed.

Miss Nelson rapped for silence. "Of course a girl can be president," she said calmly. "Are there any other nominations?"

There were none. Miss Nelson passed out white slips of paper.

"This will be a secret ballot," she said. "Please write your choice, fold the paper, and hand it to Donna Martin."

There was a buzz of whispering from most of the children. But from the back of the room Joey's friends talked loudly as they tried to persuade the children to vote for him. The ballots finally were handed to Donna, one of Holly's playmates, who had big, brown eyes and dimples.

"Please read them, Donna," Miss Nelson requested.

The seven-year-old girl opened the ballots, making two piles of papers—one for Joey, one for Pam.

The children listened eagerly as she read them off. Finally each candidate had twelve votes apiece. There was only one vote left to open!

Donna looked up at Miss Nelson a bit fearfully.

"This one will decide who's president," she quavered.

CHAPTER 3

President Pam

EVERYBODY in the Pet Club was silent as Donna Martin opened the last ballot. This would decide whether Joey Brill or Pam Hollister would be the club's president.

When Donna opened the slip of paper a big smile came over her face and she put the vote on Pam's pile. Shouts of joy from some and murmurs of grumbling from others filled the room.

"Good for you, Sis!" Pete Hollister grinned.

Joey Brill jumped up and stormed to the front of the room.

"If a girl's going to be president, I'm getting out!" he cried.

Holly giggled. "Good riddance!" she said under her breath.

"What does Pam Hollister know about pets, anyway?" Joey went on.

"She knows plenty!" Ricky defended his sister. "We have a dog, a mother cat, and five kittens, and all of them love Pam."

Miss Nelson picked up a ruler and rapped on the desk for silence. "Pam Hollister has been elected president of the Pet Club," she said. "Joey, we'd like you to remain. Perhaps you'd run for secretary."

"Not me," the boy said, glowering. "Being secretary is a sissy job."

"That isn't true, Joey," said Miss Nelson. "'There are many fine men who are secretaries in the Cabinet of our United States Government."

Joey slunk back to his seat and said no more.

"I nominate Dave Mead to be secretary," called out eight-year-old Jeff Hunter.

"Second the motion!" Holly added quickly.

Joey Brill and his friends were so angry at his losing the election for president that they did not nominate anybody to be secretary and Dave won easily. Miss Nelson gave Dave a notebook in which to write down a report of the meeting. Then the

Joey slunk back to his seat.

teacher explained what the club members would do.

"Each of you will select an animal to study," she said.

"I want to study horses!" Donna spoke up.

"And hamsters for me," Dave said.

Holly and Ricky whispered to each other. Then the red-haired boy raised his hand.

"May my sister and I study raccoons, Miss Nelson?" he asked.

"You surely may," she replied. Then she looked toward the back of the room. "Joey, what would you like to study?"

"I wanted to study raccoons," he said, scowling.

"If you wanted to take raccoons, you should have spoken sooner. Now, Joey, what other animal would you prefer?"

"A donkey!" Ricky said impishly.

Several children giggled and Joey's face became very red.

"I'll get you for saying that, Ricky Hollister!" he shouted.

"There's nothing wrong with studying donkeys," Miss Nelson said, trying to make peace, but her patience was tried to the breaking point.

"He can't call me a donkey and get away with it!" Joey exclaimed.

"Ricky didn't say any such thing," Miss Nelson said evenly. "Joey, if you can't behave yourself, you may leave!"

As the other children snickered, Joey realized he

Had Pete said something wrong?

had had enough of the argument. He lapsed into a sullen silence, casting mean looks at the Hollisters.

Pete was next to speak up for a pet. "Pam and I would like to study about Eskimo dogs, Miss Nelson," he said. "We saw the Trappers' Carnival on TV."

At this request, an expression of sadness came over the teacher's face. She gazed out the window, a far-away look in her eyes. Pete and Pam stared at each other, mystified. Had the boy said something wrong?

"Is—is it all right if we study Eskimo dogs?" Pete continued.

"Why—uh, yes. Perfectly all right," Miss Nelson said, turning back quickly.

She added that Eskimo Huskies were wonderful animals and the Hollisters would have fun studying them. One by one the other children selected animals. Joey Brill, the last to raise his hand, said he would take polar bears.

Finally the meeting ended. As the Pet Club members left the classroom, Joey tried to trip Ricky, but he jumped nimbly over the mean boy's foot and scampered away.

Next morning when the pupils in Miss Nelson's class assembled, they were surprised to find that the teacher was not there.

"I wonder if she's ill," Pam whispered to her friend, Ann Hunter.

She had hardly finished saying this when the door opened and Mr. Russell, the principal, walked in.

"Word has been received that Miss Nelson is ill," he said. "I have been telephoning to locate a substitute teacher but no one is available. I shall probably combine your class with another one later."

Pam Hollister rose from her seat and walked up to the principal.

"Mr. Russell," she said, "my mother used to be a schoolteacher. Perhaps she can help out."

The man's eyes brightened. "Fine, fine," he said. "I'll telephone her immediately."

"There's only one thing," said Pam. "I have a little sister at home. Sue's only four. Mother wouldn't have anyone to leave her with."

Mr. Russell smiled. "We'll put Sue in the kindergarten."

The principal asked Pam if she would take roll

31

and act as monitor for a few minutes until he returned. Then he hurried from the room.

Ten minutes later Mr. Russell reappeared.

"Your mother has consented to come and help us," he said, smiling. "In the meantime I want all of you to do some studying. Get out your arithmetic books."

The pupils obeyed but two minutes after Mr. Russell had left, a boy named Will Wilson, who had voted for Joey Brill, looked up. The silence in the room was suddenly disturbed as he called out sneeringly:

"The monitor's a teacher's pet! Ho ho! She's the head pet of the Pet Club!"

A couple of Joey's other backers laughed. Pam Hollister was angry, and Ann was too. She rose from

"Pam's a teacher's pet!"

her seat and started for Will's desk. Pam was fearful. She did not want her friend to get in trouble on her account.

"Ann, please sit down," the young monitor begged. "And Will, you'd better keep still or Mr. Russell will make us all stay after school."

"Aw, who cares?" Will said.

Nevertheless, he kept quiet. Will had a newspaper delivery route and did not want to be late for it. Ann sat down.

A short time later Mrs. Hollister appeared at the door. "Hello, Mother," Pam said, getting up. "Did Sue go to the kindergarten?"

Mrs. Hollister nodded yes. Then Pam introduced her to the other pupils. They all rose and said good morning.

After they had taken their seats again, the children became exceptionally quiet. They liked Mrs. Hollister immediately and even the most fidgety ones tried hard to be attentive.

After the arithmetic period was over, the new teacher asked how many of the children had seen the Trappers' Carnival on television. As several raised their hands, Pam was reminded of Miss Nelson and the sad look that had come over her face when Pete had mentioned Eskimo dogs.

Talk turned to the wonderful animals which had saved so many lives in the Far North by carrying food and medicine to people lost in blizzards.

"Huskies can stand very intense cold," Mrs. Hollister said. "And they can live for long periods on a small amount of food—just some dried fish washed down with a gulp of snow. A good team of these dogs can draw a load of hundreds of pounds forty or more miles a day over smooth snow."

"Wow!" said several of the boys.

The new teacher now turned to the reading for the day. As the pupils found their places, there came a sudden rap on the door.

"Come in," Mrs. Hollister called, but nobody appeared.

She left the desk and went to the door. Upon opening it, she found two men standing outside. One was tall and heavily built; the other short and slight. Both were rough and unpleasant-looking.

The rough men startled Mrs. Hollister.

"Is there something I can do for you?" Mrs. Hollister asked the men.

"Yes, Miss Nelson, we want to ask you some questions," the short one said gruffly. "Step out here!"

"But I'm not Miss Nelson," Mrs. Hollister told them. "She's ill today and I'm taking her place."

The men looked at each other. "Okay," said the heavy-set one in a deep, unfriendly voice. "We'll be back!"

The men turned and hurried down the corridor without saying another word. Pam was worried. Since these rough characters did not seem to know Miss Nelson, what could they have wanted of her?

Miss Nelson was becoming more mysterious every minute!

After the reading lesson was over, Mrs. Hollister said to the class, "How would you like to discuss winter sports?"

"Oh yes, please!" the pupils cried, and a girl named Carol said she had an uncle who was a wonderful skier. He could jump off high platforms and never tumble.

"Huh! That's nothing," Will Wilson scoffed. "My cousin Randy won a bobsled race at Sun Valley!"

"Why, Will," exclaimed Mrs. Hollister, "how thrilling! Won't you tell us about it?"

"Uh—well, there's not much to tell," Will stammered. "He just won it, that's all. He was the

35

driver, see—and he and the other guys on his team raced down a big, long track. Must have been fifty miles long! Another sled jumped over the embankment. My cousin's sled, No. 56B, just whizzed around them and won. Boy, was it exciting!"

"Have you any pictures you could show us?" asked Mrs. Hollister.

"Uh—well, no—that is, I just read about it in the paper," Will finished lamely.

"I'll say he read about it!" A boy named Don Wells spoke up. "It was in *Exciting Comics* last month—'Adventures of Randy Wilson'!"

"What do you mean, Don?" Mrs. Hollister asked.

"I'll bet he just made it up from that story in the magazine!"

All the children gasped, and turned to stare at Will.

"Is this true, Will?" Mrs. Hollister began, but just at that moment, the children heard a giggle and running footsteps in the corridor.

A moment later the door flew open. In ran Sue Hollister! Her face was smeared with red and black paint like an Indian's.

"Mommy!" she cried, skipping over to Mrs. Hollister. "I'm an Indian and I got away from our camp!"

The pupils burst out laughing.

"Sue!" Mrs. Hollister exclaimed. "Where did you get that paint?"

"We were finger painting," Sue answered.

"Mommy! I'm an Indian!"

" 'Member when we saw the Indians out West? They finger painted their faces, didn't they, Mommy?"

This remark made the pupils laugh all the harder. One mischievous boy said, "Can you dance like an Indian?"

Before Mrs. Hollister could restrain Sue, the little girl put a hand to her mouth, let out a war whoop, and began to dance around in a circle.

"Sue, stop it!" Mrs. Hollister pleaded. "I'm afraid the whole school will hear you and there'll be trouble."

Just then other footsteps sounded in the corridor. The children stopped laughing but they were concerned. If this were Principal Russell, he might make Mrs. Hollister leave at once. They did not want this to happen!

CHAPTER 4

Fun and Excitement

Too late Sue quieted down and looked wide-eyed at her mother. She knew she should have stayed in the kindergarten and not played Indian in the classroom where Mrs. Hollister was the substitute teacher.

"I'll behave, Mommy," she promised. "Honest Injun!"

Everyone listened intently as the footsteps approached the door. Somebody must have complained about the laughter caused by Sue's antics!

When the door finally opened, everyone breathed a sigh of relief. There stood Miss Rankin, the kindergarten teacher. She was a young woman with dark hair and a cheerful, round face.

"So there you are," she said, looking at Sue. "I thought I'd find you with your mother."

"I'm awful sorry," Sue apologized.

Miss Rankin held up some paper towels to wipe the paint from Sue's face.

"It's too bad my daughter caused you all this trouble, Miss Rankin," said Mrs. Hollister.

"No trouble at all," the kindergarten teacher said kindly. "Sue was telling me about the Indians she

38

She tried to hide from her teacher.

met while you were hunting for the turquoise treasure. She just wanted to look like them, I'm sure."

Miss Rankin stepped toward the little girl, but before she could wipe her face, Sue scampered down one of the aisles and wriggled into the seat next to Pam. Then she slid down as far as she could so the teacher would not see her.

"You can't hide here, Sue," her sister said, putting an arm around the little girl.

"Come up here, dear," Mrs. Hollister insisted.

Sue slid out of the seat and walked to the front of the room. As Miss Rankin led her from the room, Sue turned and waved to everybody in the class. "We got a burro out West named Sunday," she said. "When he comes to our house, I'll bring him to school!"

After the children stopped laughing, Mrs. Hollister once more turned to her teaching. For ten minutes the pupils paid strict attention to their spelling recitation. Will was in the middle of the word "project" when without warning, the door, which had not been tightly closed, swung open with a bang. The children burst into laughter as a big, brown-haired dog sprang into the room.

"Zip!" Pam shouted.

It was the Hollisters' beautiful collie. Zip bounded down the aisle to his young mistress and licked one of Pam's hands.

"How did you get in school?" she asked, patting him affectionately. "Was the janitor's door open?"

The collie lifted his head and gave a soft whine.

"Zip's like Mary's lamb," said Ann Hunter. "He followed Pam to school one day and made the children laugh—but not play."

Mrs. Hollister looked at the clock. "Well, it will soon be time to play, children," she said. She added that Zip might remain in the classroom until recess, when the children went outside for their games. Then he would have to go home.

"Zip, come up here and lie down!" she commanded.

The collie walked to the front of the room and lay down near the teacher's desk. He closed one eye but kept the other open to watch Mrs. Hollister. Evidently he could not figure out why she was there.

His action amused the new teacher, who smiled

and said, "If Mr. Hollister were here, our whole family would be in school."

"Except our cat, White Nose, and her kittens," Pam laughed.

At this moment Joey Brill came storming into the room, waving a big stick in his right hand.

"Where's that dog?" he shouted. "Oh, there he is. Come here! Get out of school!"

As Joey ran toward Zip, the dog got up and scooted back beside Pam. Joey raised the stick as if to hit the whimpering animal, but Pam sprang up and wrested it from him.

"Don't you dare!" she said. "It's unkind to hit animals."

"Your dog has no right in our school," Joey said, "and I'm going to drive him out. Mr. Russell told me to."

"Don't you dare hit my dog!"

"You'll not do it with a stick," Mrs. Hollister said angrily. She had followed Joey and now grabbed his arm. "If Mr. Russell wants Zip to leave, we'll see that he gets out of the building. Pam, please lead Zip outside and tell him to go home."

"Yes, Mother," Pam replied, getting out of her seat and heading for the door. "Come on, Zip, let's go!"

She led the dog down the corridor and out the front door of the school. Joey followed menacingly but did not try to hit Zip again.

"Now go home, Zip," Pam ordered, "and stay there until we get back."

The dog looked up into the face of his mistress. Then he started off through the school yard and Pam returned to the classroom. As she passed Ann Hunter's seat, the girl whispered:

"We never had so much fun with a substitute teacher before. I hope your mother will be here a long time."

Pam smiled. She thought her mother was a very good teacher, but Pam knew Mrs. Hollister could not remain very many days at the school. When would Miss Nelson return? And were those rough-looking men connected with why she had looked so sad when Eskimo dogs were mentioned?

Mrs. Hollister continued with the lesson until the bell rang for recess. After Pam had slipped into her jacket, she went to give her mother's hand a squeeze and then ran out to the school yard.

The older boys and girls had obtained a soft ball and bat from the gymnasium. Now they were ready to pick sides for a game.

"I'll be captain of one team," Joey Brill announced, gathering a few of his friends about him.

"Pete, you take the other," Dave Mead called out, and several of the children said, "Yeah!"

"Okay," Pete said. "I'll challenge you, Joey."

The two captains selected boys and girls, until the sides were even at nine apiece.

"My team's up first," Joey said importantly.

"Let's twirl for first licks," Pete suggested.

When Joey grudgingly consented to this, Pete picked up a bat and tossed it to him. Joey grabbed it at the base with one hand. Pete put a hand above his on the handle, then Joey another still higher. This

Pete grasped the top.

43

kept on until there was only room enough for Pete to grasp the top in his finger tips.

"Three times around your head without dropping it and our side's up first!" shouted Pam. Her brother had picked her to play second base.

Pete carefully twirled the bat around his head, once, twice. It almost slipped from his fingers! Three times!

His teammates shouted approval and there was nothing the glowering Joey could do about it. The other children in the playground gathered around as Pete's team went to bat first.

Amid much whistling and shouting, first one side and then the other whacked the ball about the playground. Before the fifteen-minute recess was over, Pete's team was ahead seven runs to six.

"Come on, we'll get 'em now," Joey said as his team prepared for their last time at bat.

One of Joey's teammates hit a home run and the score was tied. Now it was Joey's turn at the plate. Before he could take a swing at the ball, the school bell rang. As the children started to hurry back to the classroom, Joey said:

"Hey, wait until I hit the ball!" But the players ignored him. Joey was so angry that he threw his bat to the ground and stormed off.

"I'm going to get even with you Hollisters!" he yelled when Pete headed for the gymnasium to return the baseball equipment.

Pete paid no attention. He was used to Joey's

threats. But as he was walking toward his room a few minutes later he heard someone say, "Oh boy, Ricky Hollister's going to get it!" and wondered what was wrong.

As Pete hurried toward a group in the hallway, he noticed that a strong stream of water was squirting from one of the drinking fountains. The floor was being flooded.

"What happened?" Pete asked, trying to turn off the water but unable to do it.

"The fountain's stuck!" someone said.

Pete leaned over it and exclaimed, "Someone pushed a match stick in the nozzle. Quick, call the janitor to bring a pail."

Dave Mead, who was standing near by, ran off while Pete took a pen knife from his pocket. He dug at the match stick, getting all wet himself. Finally the last bit of it flew from the nozzle like a shot and the water turned off.

"Who did this?" Pete asked.

"I know," said a girl standing near by. "Ricky Hollister!"

Pete turned to face her. She was Alma Brown.

"My brother did this?" he said unbelievingly.

"Yes," Alma replied.

Just then Mr. Logan, the janitor, came down the hall, carrying a mop and pail. He was followed by Mr. Russell.

"What's going on here?" the principal said as Mr. Logan began to sop up the water.

"Ricky Hollister put a match stick in the drinking fountain." Alma spoke up quickly.

Mr. Russell looked sternly at Pete. "Did you know about this?"

"No, sir."

Without another word the principal turned and strode back to his office.

Ricky, meanwhile, had returned to his room after the ball game and was in his seat when the telephone rang alongside his teacher's desk. She picked up the receiver.

"Yes, yes, he's here," she said. "Do you want him right away? All right, Mr. Russell." The teacher turned and looked at Ricky. "You're wanted in the office immediately," she said.

Ricky did not know why he was wanted. Perhaps Mr. Russell would send him on an errand somewhere. He hurried out of the room. When he arrived at the office, Mr. Russell said:

"Ricky, take a seat over there."

The boy sat down and looked at the principal, who seemed very severe.

"I'm surprised and disappointed in you, Ricky," the principal said. "I never thought you would play a trick that would damage the school."

Ricky grew worried as he gazed at the principal. What was Mr. Russell talking about?

"I don't understand what you mean," Ricky said as tears started to fill his eyes.

"I think you do," the principal said. "Alma Brown

saw you plug up the drinking fountain. The water flooded the corridor. If it hadn't been noticed in time, there might have been serious damage. You'll have to be punished for this!"

CHAPTER 5

Fighting a Bully

Ricky Hollister's lower lip quivered as he looked straight at the principal.

"Mr. Russell, I didn't do it," he said. "I wasn't even near the drinking fountain today."

The principal picked up his telephone and called Ricky's teacher. He asked her whether the boy had left the room that morning except at recess time.

"No, Mr. Russell."

Then he inquired whether Ricky had come straight from the playground after recess.

"Yes, he did."

The principal hung up the phone and turned to Ricky.

"I don't see when you would have had a chance to plug up the fountain," he said. "Stay here a moment and I will call Alma."

Mr. Russell telephoned Alma's teacher and the girl was sent to the office. When she entered he motioned her to a chair alongside Ricky. The principal told her she must be mistaken in blaming the boy for causing the small flood in the school.

Alma seemed very nervous. She kept pulling at the

trimming on her dress and looked down at the floor. Then she said:

"Well, maybe it wasn't Ricky. But it must have been someone who looked like him."

"Why did you make up this story, Alma?" Mr. Russell asked her severely.

Alma burst into tears. "Joey Brill said Ricky did it," she wailed. "But I think Joey did it himself!"

Mr. Russell told her it was not fair to place blame on an innocent person. Then he sent her back to the classroom.

After Alma had left, Mr. Russell told Ricky he was sorry and the boy went back to his room feeling much better. A little later Pete noted that Joey was called from their classroom to the principal's office. When Joey returned, he looked pretty sober. Besides, he had to stay after school an hour for his prank.

On the way home Pete told Pam what had happened.

"Serves Joey right for telling Alma a fib to pass along and get Ricky into trouble," Pam declared.

She and Pete expected Joey to be nice to the Hollisters after that at least for a while. How surprised Pam was when at four-thirty he marched into their back yard, where she was playing with Zip. The boy had a mean, triumphant look on his face. Smirking, he walked up to her.

"I just found out that you aren't president of the Pet Club after all," he said. "I'm the president and I can prove it!"

"I'm the president, not you!" Joey declared.

"What do you mean?" Pam asked in amazement. "The ballots were counted and I won by one vote."

"The ballots weren't counted right," Joey protested. "Your friend Donna doesn't know how to add!"

"How do you know?" Pam asked quickly. "Did you open Miss Nelson's desk and count them again?"

Joey's face turned beet red. "I—I," he stammered. "Of course not. I went around and asked different people how they voted. I had at least fifteen!"

Pam was stunned. Maybe Donna had made a mistake! How embarrassing!

"I'll take charge of the first meeting," Joey announced, and walked off.

Poor Pam! She wanted to cry but held back the tears.

She hurried into the house and dialed Miss Nelson's number. She heard the phone ring and ring but no one answered.

"Oh dear!" Pam said. Then she brightened. If Miss Nelson was not at home, she must be feeling better and would be at school next day. Pam would go early and ask her.

After Pam hung up, she ran to the kitchen, where her mother was preparing supper. When Mrs. Hollister heard the story, she put an arm around her daughter.

"Don't feel too bad, dear, if you're not the president," she said. "If a mistake has been made and Joey was really elected, then he deserves the position."

"I know, Mother," Pam said sadly. "But I don't see how Donna could have made such a mistake."

Pam continued to worry about it as she set the table. In the living room the younger children were watching the television weather news. The announcer at the local station stood before a big chart. In a moment he pointed to lower Canada and said it was growing cold in this area.

"That's where Gram and Gramp are." Ricky spoke up. "Oh boy, when we go up there, we'll sure have to wear warm clothes."

"Listen!" Holly commanded.

"A long cold spell," the weatherman went on, "is expected to hit this part of the country in about a week. Residents of Shoreham and vicinity can look for extremely low temperatures and snow."

"I must find out whether Joey was right."

The screen showed a picture of a man covered with icicles and the children laughed.

"Br-r-r!" said Holly, hunching her shoulders and wrapping her arms around herself.

"I'm an icicle girl," Sue announced.

"Look out! You'll melt by that radiator!" Ricky teased.

Pam took little interest in either the weather or the joking. She was still fretting over the outcome of the Pet Club election.

Next morning she was the first one up, the first to finish breakfast, and the first to start for school.

"My goodness, you're full of energy today," Mrs. Hollister said as she kissed Pam good-by.

"Oh, Mother, I simply must find out whether Joey was right about the election," she said, and hurried off.

Pam was at the school before the doors were opened. When Mr. Logan let the pupils in, she hurried to her room.

Miss Nelson was not there yet. Pam, wondering whether her mother would be called to substitute again, went to her seat. But just before the bell rang, Miss Nelson appeared. How glad Pam was to see that the teacher seemed to be feeling all right. There was no time to talk to her, though, before lessons started.

Pam waited patiently until recess time. She was just about to speak to the teacher when Joey Brill hurried into the room.

"Miss Nelson, Miss Nelson!" he said excitedly, and began to talk quickly in low tones.

Joey whispered to the teacher.

The teacher pulled open her desk drawer and took out two piles of little papers.

The Pet Club ballots!

Pam could stand the suspense no longer. She hurried to the front of the room.

"Miss Nelson, Joey says that I'm not president of the club. Is that right?"

With this Joey picked up one of the piles. "These have my name on them," he said. "Look yourself, Pam, and count them."

Her hands trembling, Pam picked up the pile, looked at the name on each slip, and counted them. Fifteen votes for Joey Brill! That meant Pam had had only ten instead of thirteen.

"Ha, ha, I told you so," Joey said as he put the piles back in the desk and then left the room.

Tears welled into Pam's eyes. She bit her lip and returned to her seat, where she buried her head in her arms. Miss Nelson walked over to Pam and put her hand on the girl's shoulder.

"Don't worry, dear," she said. "We all make mistakes. I dare say Donna will feel even worse than you do."

Pam admitted this but she was so upset that she did not even go out for recess. When lunch time came she could hardly eat, although her family tried to cheer her up. Word spread around the school quickly that Donna had counted the ballots wrong and that Joey Brill was president of the Pet Club.

"I feel terrible," Donna said when she met Pam

in the corridor ten minutes before the bell for afternoon classes rang. Pam could see that the girl had been crying.

Just then Pete Hollister ran up to them. "I think Joey's up to one of his tricks," he said. "I watched very closely when Donna was counting the votes. I'm sure you won, Pam. Did Miss Nelson count your votes again?"

Pam did not think Miss Nelson had, but why was this necessary? There were only twenty-five altogether.

Pam and Donna went to their rooms but Pete hurried to the school yard to play for a few minutes before the afternoon session started. The first person he met outside was Joey Brill.

"Take that back!"

"Yah, yah," Joey taunted, "your sister got Donna to cheat with the ballots. But Pam didn't win the election!"

Pete was furious. "You take that back!" he demanded. "If there was a mistake in the counting, it was not because my sister is a cheat."

"Yes she is, yes she is. She's a meanie!" Joey insisted.

Pete clenched his fists. "Take that back!"

"I will not!"

With a quick jab, Pete hit Joey on the nose. The bigger boy teetered back, regained his balance, and came at Pete with both fists flying. For a few moments there was a melee of arms and legs.

The boys fell to the ground, their arms wrapped about each other. First Pete was on top, then Joey rolled over and gained the advantage.

The other children in the school yard, including Ricky Hollister, gathered around. Pete's jacket was torn open and the cuff of Joey's shirt was ripped. The fighters' hair was mussed and their faces dirty as they rolled over and over.

"You—take—that back!" Pete said, panting.

"I never will!" Joey replied, scrambling to his feet.

Although Pete was smaller than his rival, he was quicker. With a sudden movement he got a headlock on Joey, and with a quick twist threw the boy to the ground. Then Pete flung himself on top of Joey, kneeling on Joey's arms with both knees. The larger boy could not move.

"Hey fellas, help me!" Joey shouted.

Pete looked down into Joey's face. "Have you had enough?" he asked.

Joey winced and nodded.

"Do you take back what you said about Pam?"

"Y-yes, yes."

"Then say she's not a cheat," Pete insisted.

"All right, she's not a cheat," Joey said.

Just then three boys came running from the school building and elbowed their way through the ring of children. Pete recognized them immediately as friends of Joey's. The beaten boy saw them, too.

"Hey, fellas, help me!" he shouted.

The boys dashed toward Pete Hollister, who quickly jumped off Joey and turned to meet the rush. Joey hit him from behind, as the other three flung themselves at Pete!

CHAPTER 6

A Mean Trick

"STOP! Stop!" Ricky shouted when he saw his brother being pummeled by Joey and three of his friends.

As he rushed to Pete's aid, other children quickly pitched in and helped pull the four boys off Pete Hollister. Outnumbered, they ran away, but Joey called back:

"Guess that'll teach you, Pete!"

"Who were those mean boys with Joey?" Ricky asked his brother, as Pete arose and brushed off his clothes.

"I don't know their names."

Suddenly Pete snapped his fingers. *Three boys! Three votes!* Had Joey used these friends to write his name on three extra ballots and slip them into Miss Nelson's desk? Pete was determined to find out.

Without telling the rest of his family, he got in touch with Dave after school and told him what he suspected.

"Joey said he asked people who voted. How about you and I doing the same thing?"

The teacher counted the ballots herself.

"Okay," Dave agreed. "I sure hope Joey isn't president."

The boys hopped onto their bicycles and visited the homes of all those they were sure had put Pam's name on their ballots. Everyone had. Next Pete and Dave started on the rest of the list. Half an hour later they had contacted all these.

Pam had thirteen votes!

"She's president!" Dave shouted. "Let's go get Joey and make him pay for this!"

Pete wanted to but thought perhaps Miss Nelson should be told first. Anyway, Pam ought to know at once.

How excited she was to hear the good news! But she insisted they must be absolutely sure and made the boys agree to keep it a secret until all the ballots had been counted by Miss Nelson.

Pam and the boys went to school early next morning. Miss Nelson was there correcting notebooks.

"Good morning," she said.

The children said good morning, and at once Pam told her what the boys had found out.

Miss Nelson looked surprised. "You mean there may be three extra votes?" she asked unbelievingly.

"Yes, and they're for Joey," Pete replied.

The teacher quickly opened her desk and counted the ballots herself. Fifteen for Joey, thirteen for Pam!

"Why, that's twenty-eight and as I recall only twenty-five joined the club," Miss Nelson said, perplexed.

"I think three of Joey's friends wrote his name on extra ballots and Joey put them in your desk after school," Pete stated. He sorted the papers. "See," he said. "Three of these don't match the other slips."

"I guess that's proof enough," Miss Nelson said. "Thank you for telling me about this. Pam, a great injustice has been done to you. I'll see that the whole matter is straightened out this morning. I have just one request. Let the school authorities punish Joey. Don't you children try to do it."

She left the room immediately, and a little later, when the whole class had assembled, the teacher announced that Pam was president of the Pet Club. At assembly Mr. Russell made the same statement and all Pam's friends smiled at her.

"Pet Club members," he went on, "are invited to come to the school library after classes today to study about their favorite animals. Miss Allen, our librarian, will help you."

Pete, Pam, Ricky, and Holly met in the library after school was over. It was very quiet.

Miss Allen, a kind-faced woman with gray hair, had animal books spread out on the long table in the middle of the room. Ricky and Holly picked out a big illustrated book about raccoons. Pete and Pam each chose one on Eskimo dogs.

"Pete," Pam said presently in a low tone, "do you know there are ever so many kinds of arctic dogs?"

"And," Pete broke in, "they all have thick coats and tough feet. Gee! it says here they look sort of like wolves around their eyes."

"Oh, they can't be too gentle, then," declared Pam. But a moment later she read, " 'Sled dogs are really friendly!' "

Pam was so intent upon her reading that she did not notice a child walk softly into the library and approach her. When the girl felt a little hand touch hers, she turned around, startled.

"Sue, what are you doing here!" Pam exclaimed.

Sue Hollister's rosy face broke into a dimpled smile. "I like school. Mother said I could come back. Can't I stay here with you?"

Pam smiled at her little sister. "All right."

"Listen to this." Pete spoke up. "It's believed that Eskimo dogs lived originally in Siberia and were brought to this continent 2,000 years ago."

"You open it, Sis."

In a loud voice Sue asked, "How can dogs be 2,000 years old?"

Pam and Pete laughed softly and Pam said, "Shh, Sue! Don't forget to whisper, or you'll have to go home."

At the supper table that evening, talk turned to Pete's and Pam's study of Eskimo dogs.

"I was in the library too," Sue announced in a tiny whisper.

"You were where?" Mr. Hollister asked. "Speak up, I can hardly hear you."

"Daddy," Sue said, still in a whisper, "when you're talking about the library you're s'posed to whisper!"

Everyone laughed, then Ricky asked if Gram and Gramp Hollister had any Eskimo dogs.

"No," his father replied, "but some of their neighbors do. It's a great honor to have a winning team in the Trappers' Carnival. Any puppies of those Huskies are bought by the Canadian Mounted Police."

"Do they pull the Mounties' sleds?" Holly asked.

"Exactly. And the Mounties want the fastest dogs in all Canada."

Just then the door bell rang.

"I'll answer it," Pete offered. A moment later he called, "It's a special-delivery letter—from Froston!"

As Pete ran back to the dining room, he said, "It's addressed to Pam. You open it, Sis."

Breathlessly the Hollisters waited to hear the message from Gram and Gramp. Pam unfolded the letter.

"It's from Gram and says:

"Gramp and I were so happy to hear from you and were glad you enjoyed the Trappers' Carnival on television. We would love to have you come and visit us over the Thanksgiving week end. Fortunately the people who had rented our largest cottage have canceled their reservation, so you may have it."

"Oh goody, goody!" Holly cried gleefully, bouncing up and down in her chair.

"The letter isn't finished yet," Pam said. She went on reading:

"Your parents may bring you up any time during Thanksgiving week. We'll have lots of fun together.

Love from both of us,
Gram."

"Crickets!" Pete exclaimed. "I can hardly wait!"

"Yikes!" Ricky cried. "Now we can see the dog race!"

"I hope Fluff runs this time," said Pam.

"We're all very lucky there was room for us at Snowflake Camp," Mrs. Hollister smiled.

With the prospect of the delightful trip before them, the children found it hard to fall asleep that night. But finally each one did. Next morning before class began Pam told Miss Nelson of her grand-parents' invitation.

"Isn't that splendid!" the teacher replied enthusi-astically.

"I'll be able to see real Eskimo dogs up there," Pam said.

"I have a surprise for the Pet Club."

At once Miss Nelson stopped smiling. A note of sadness crept into her voice as she said, "That's certainly the best way to learn about Huskies."

"Don't—don't you like Eskimo dogs?" Pam asked.

"Why yes, of course I do, dear," Miss Nelson said. "You see——" The teacher did not finish the sentence. Instead she said in a more cheerful voice:

"I have a surprise for you. The Pet Club members have been invited to visit Dr. Wesley's animal hospital. He's a veterinarian, you know."

"How wonderful!" said Pam. "When may we go?"

"This afternoon." Miss Nelson requested Pam to tell the others in the club about the trip. "We'll meet at my classroom right after school."

At the appointed time, most of the club members, including Joey Brill, joined the Hollister children in front of Miss Nelson's room. They set out at once for Dr. Wesley's office, which was not far away.

What a bright and gleaming office it was! At once the children heard puppies whimpering and kittens mewing.

Just then Dr. Wesley, a tall man with silver-gray hair, came in. He shook hands with each of the Pet Club members and said he was glad they were so interested in learning more about animals.

"You'll be particularly interested in a special dog I have here," he said.

He beckoned the group to follow him out a rear door into a large back yard. A long row of kennels was arranged about the yard. The children bent down to see the dogs and cats in their little houses.

In one kennel was a Chihuahua—a tiny Mexican dog. Next door, looking huger than ever in contrast to his little neighbor, was a great Dane.

Holly looked up at Dr. Wesley. "And where is the special dog?" she asked, twirling one of her pigtails.

Dr. Wesley indicated a kennel on the opposite side of the yard which had a fenced-in run back of it. Eagerly the children ran to it and peered over the fence. There stood one of the most beautiful dogs the Hollisters had ever seen.

"A *Husky!*" breathed Pam admiringly.

"Yes," said Dr. Wesley, "he's one of the finest of his breed. His name is Jack."

Jack, Pam observed, was buff-colored and held his

"Here's Jack, the Eskimo dog."

plumed tail curled over his back—just as she had read that Huskies do.

"He sure doesn't look sick," Ricky commented, puzzled.

"You're right about that," Dr. Wesley said. "In fact, he's as sound as a dollar." The veterinarian explained that Jack had been left to board by his master, who was away on a vacation of several weeks.

Pete, meanwhile, guessed that the animal was all of two feet tall. He asked Dr. Wesley how much Jack weighed.

"About eighty-five pounds," was the reply. "All muscle, too—not a spare ounce of fat."

Dr. Wesley slipped a strong leash on Jack and led him out of the kennel. How friendly and gentle the dog was as all the children patted him! After Pete walked the beautiful animal around the yard a few times, Dr. Wesley returned Jack to his kennel.

"I hope the Eskimo dogs at Froston are as nice as Jack," said Pam, and told of the dog-sled race she and her brothers and sisters would see at Thanksgiving.

Dr. Wesley said they were lucky—the Trappers' Carnival was very exciting. He added, "If it's a warm day and the snow is slushy, the dogs had better wear boots."

"Boots?" repeated all the children at once.

The veterinarian explained that Eskimo dogs wore tiny leather boots when the snow started to melt. Otherwise balls of ice might form between their toes and hurt them.

"This can be mighty serious sometimes," Dr. Wesley said. "Many a lead dog has stumbled and mixed up a whole team because of it."

Pam whispered to Pete, "Maybe that's why Fluff lost the race."

"Dr. Wesley," Holly said, "my brother Ricky and I have been studying about raccoons."

"I'm glad you told me that," the veterinarian replied. "I'm treating a pet raccoon. Some children found it at camp last summer. I'll show it to you."

He led the way to another cage. All the visitors followed him except Joey Brill, who hung back a little. As the group passed a cage with very strong bars, the doctor warned:

"Don't stand too close to this kennel. There's a mean dog in it, and he's likely to be irritated by people getting near him."

Just then he stopped in front of a small cage and reached inside. He brought out the cutest raccoon the children had ever seen. What bright little eyes! And what a pretty, bushy tail!

"Her name is Betsy," Dr. Wesley said, setting the raccoon on the ground. "She can do all sorts of clever tricks."

As the children watched, fascinated, Betsy swayed back and forth, then rolled over in a triple somersault.

All the Pet Club members but one clapped in delight. Joey Brill was paying no attention to the animal's antics. He was wandering in the direction of the cage where the mean dog was kept.

The mean dog sprang from his kennel.

At this moment, Pete turned and saw Joey open the door. The dog sprang from his kennel. With a menacing growl the beast raced for the group of children!

CHAPTER 7

Ricky to the Rescue

As THE mean dog bounded toward the children barking furiously, Betsy the raccoon raced up a tree. Dr. Wesley cried out, "Stop, Dan! Stop! Back to your kennel!"

But the angry dog paid no attention. Most of the children by now had scattered in various directions, trying to get away from the animal. As he nipped at one little girl's shoes, Pam Hollister, who had not moved an inch, called to the dog softly.

"Down, Dan, be a good dog!"

She held out her hand to him in a friendly gesture.

To everybody's astonishment, the dog stopped nipping and approached Pam. When he came close enough, Pam patted his head. The next moment Dan actually started wagging his tail.

Dr. Wesley and Miss Nelson looked at each other in wonder, then gazed admiringly at Pam. She continued to speak gently to the dog. Finally, putting her fingers under his collar, she led Dan to his kennel. Once he was inside, Pam closed the door and pushed the hook into the latch.

Pete, Ricky, and Holly looked proudly at their sister as Dr. Wesley said, "You're a brave girl."

"How did you ever remain so calm?" Miss Nelson asked.

"Well," replied Pam with a little smile, "I wasn't really afraid. I just love all animals, and I guess they know it."

"That proves you've learned the secret of animal training," the veterinarian remarked.

Pam was happy to hear this. One of her fondest dreams was that someday she might raise horses and dogs.

Meanwhile, Joey Brill had been trying to sneak out of the kennel yard. But Miss Nelson spied him.

"Just a minute, Joey!" she called. "Did you let Dan out of his kennel?"

All eyes turned on the unpleasant boy. "Aw, I—I

Joey tried to sneak out.

didn't do it on purpose," he muttered. "I was just—just fooling around with the lock and my hand slipped."

Miss Nelson said this was a lame excuse. He should have stayed with the group. She declared sternly that it would be a long time before Joey would accompany the Pet Club on any excursions. Turning to the others, she said it was time for all of them to go.

"But we must rescue the little raccoon first," Holly spoke up anxiously.

"You're right," Dr. Wesley said, glancing at the pet, which had climbed to the top branch.

"How will we ever get her down?" asked Donna Martin.

Ricky had an idea. "I'll shin up and bring her down on my shoulders," the freckle-nosed boy offered.

"Thanks, but I guess you won't have to do that," Dr. Wesley said with a smile. "There's a ladder in the garage I keep handy for such emergencies."

Pete and Ricky helped him carry the long extension ladder to the yard. The doctor placed it at the foot of the tree, pulled on a rope, and the ladder stretched out twice as long. The top of it reached to the upper branches where the raccoon sat, peering down at them.

"Betsy looks as if she's laughing at us," Holly giggled.

Ricky had been eying the ladder. "May I please go up and get Betsy?" he asked the veterinarian.

Ricky rescued the raccoon.

Dr. Wesley smiled broadly. "Go ahead."

Ricky scrambled up the ladder like a monkey. Soon he reached the top branches. Steadying himself, he reached out along the limb and got hold of the raccoon.

Carefully he placed her on his shoulder and slowly descended the ladder. When Ricky stepped from the last rung onto the ground, the children cheered him.

As Dr. Wesley put Betsy back in her cage, he said, "Don't you run away again!"

He had just locked her in when his outdoor telephone rang. He walked over to the box, which was just inside a tool shed, and picked up the receiver. The children were silent as the veterinarian spoke.

He began talking about Eskimo dogs. It seemed that someone was inquiring where a purebred animal might be purchased. Dr. Wesley replied that the best breeder of Eskimo dogs had been missing for about a year.

When he said this, Pam noticed Miss Nelson walk rapidly away from the children. The teacher turned her head as if she did not want anyone to see her suddenly put a handkerchief to her eyes. Then she darted into the office.

Why, Pam wondered, was her teacher so sad every time Eskimo dogs were mentioned? The girl wished she might help the woman.

Dr. Wesley finished his conversation by saying, "If I ever hear of this Traver fellow again, I'll let you know."

Meanwhile, Pam had followed Miss Nelson, who now was seated in one of the big chairs drying her eyes.

"Is—is something wrong?" Pam asked gently.

The woman smiled faintly but did not answer the question directly. "I'm sure everything will be all right," she said. "Thank you, my dear."

But this did not convince Pam. Something was the matter! Could it have anything to do with the person named Traver Dr. Wesley had mentioned?

Pam went outside and discussed this with Pete. After the Pet Club members had thanked Dr. Wesley for having shown them the kennels and were leaving for their homes, the two children lingered behind to speak to the veterinarian.

"Would you mind telling us something about the Mr. Traver who is missing?" Pete asked.

"Is it important?" Dr. Wesley asked.

The animal doctor seemed a little surprised at the boy's question. But he smiled and said, "The man's full name is Traver Nelson."

Traver Nelson! Pam and Pete could not conceal their excitement.

"Is he related to my teacher?" Pam asked eagerly.

Dr. Wesley stroked his chin thoughtfully. "That never occurred to me," he replied. "But I doubt it. Traver Nelson lived in Canada." He looked at Pete and Pam quizzically. "Is it very important that you find out?" he queried.

A glance from Pete told his sister he thought it best not to reveal their suspicions that something might be wrong. Quickly Pam said:

"No. I was wondering why he's missing and if Miss Nelson knows this."

"I can't answer either question," the veterinarian replied.

After thanking the doctor for his information, Pete and Pam said good-by and hurried outside.

"I'll bet a cookie," Pete declared, "that this Traver Nelson *is* related to your teacher, Pam. Why don't we ask her?"

But Pam did not want to make Miss Nelson feel bad again that day. "Let's wait," she suggested. "Anyway, I'd like to tell Mother about it first and ask her advice."

Soon Pete and Pam caught up with the others and walked home with Ricky and Holly. After supper that evening Pam told Mrs. Hollister what she had in mind.

Mrs. Hollister thought a moment. "If Miss Nelson has some problem with which we can be of any assistance," she said kindly, "I certainly think we should try to help her. Suppose we invite Miss Nelson to dinner. We can talk with her then."

Pam was enthusiastic about this plan. "Will you write an invitation, Mother? I'll give it to her Monday."

Mrs. Hollister said she would do this immediately. Getting some pretty note paper from her desk, she wrote Miss Nelson, asking her to dinner Monday evening.

The next day being Saturday, the Hollisters were busy with chores in the morning and watched a football game in the afternoon on television. On Sunday, they all went to church.

Monday morning Pam was so eager to deliver the note, she could hardly wait for school to begin. But finally she placed the invitation on the teacher's desk. A smile crossed Miss Nelson's face as she read it.

"Thank you so much for the invi——" she started to say, when a voice called rudely from the doorway:

"Teacher's pet! Teacher's pet!"

Pam turned in time to see that her taunter was Joey Brill, but he dashed from sight before Miss Nelson saw who it was. The teacher went on:

"It was very sweet of your mother to invite me to dinner. I'll be most happy to accept!"

"Oh, I'm so glad," Pam said happily, and secretly she said to herself, "I hope we can help you."

Miss Nelson wrote a reply, saying she would be at the Hollisters' promptly at seven. That evening at quarter to seven, Ricky Hollister stood before the tall mirror in the hallway. He was trying to plaster down a cowlick in his hair that would not stay put. His brother and sisters were all neatly dressed, and waiting eagerly for Miss Nelson.

Pam rushed to open the door and Miss Nelson entered. After everyone had chatted gaily for a few minutes, Mrs. Hollister said that dinner was ready.

During the meal Pam was pleased to notice that Miss Nelson seemed to be enjoying herself very much. Talk finally turned to the school's Pet Club and the Hollisters learned that the teacher had been

77

The teacher was startled by Pam's question.

chosen to be the club adviser because she knew a good deal about animals.

The teacher said she knew quite a lot about them. She loved dogs, and as a matter of fact, her father used to raise them.

"Any particular kind?" Pete asked.

Miss Nelson became pensive. She looked down at her plate and was silent for a few moments. Then finally she said:

"We—we raised Eskimo dogs."

The Hollisters sensed that what the teacher had just told them had something to do with her feeling of sadness at times. Pam was the first to speak. "Miss Nelson," she said, "is the missing man named Traver Nelson related to you?"

The teacher was startled by the girl's question, and her face showed great consternation. Then Miss Nelson looked directly at Pam.

"Traver," she said, "is my twin brother."

CHAPTER 8

The Teacher's Strange Story

UPON hearing the teacher's announcement, the Hollisters gasped. Traver Nelson, the missing Eskimo dog expert, was her twin brother! No wonder she was sad!

"You have no idea where he is?" asked Pam.

Miss Nelson sighed. "I wish I did," she said wistfully. After a pause she added, "If you would like to hear it, I'll tell you the whole story."

"Oh, please do," Pam urged, and all the Hollisters nodded.

"Several years ago," Miss Nelson began, "my brother moved to Canada, where he carried on our family's lifelong interest—breeding fine Eskimo dogs, especially racers."

When the teacher paused for a moment, Ricky remarked, "That's good."

Miss Nelson smiled faintly. "Yes, Ricky, it was very good—until last year."

Then she told the Hollisters that the previous year something very strange had happened. Traver had entered the dog-sled race of the Trappers' Carnival. He

79

had lost it because of a cruel trick someone had played on him.

"You mean the race where Fluff was the lead dog?" Pam asked excitedly. "We saw that on television."

"Yes, that was Traver's team," Miss Nelson replied.

"The poor doggie Fluff hurt herself," Sue piped up.

Miss Nelson nodded and gave another sigh. "Yes, the snow turned to slush and my brother had put boots on Fluff. But when he wasn't looking, somebody took them off. So when ice caked between her toes, she stumbled and lost the race."

The Hollisters looked at one another in dismay. Who could be so mean as to hurt a gentle, beautiful creature like Fluff!

"Your brother disappeared!"

"It was a shame," the teacher went on. "Fluff was such a wonderful king dog, too."

"A *king* dog?" Pete echoed. "I thought Fluff was a lady dog."

This made Miss Nelson chuckle in spite of her worries. "She is indeed a lady," the teacher said. "But the leader of a Husky team is always called a king dog or a lead dog."

"She's a queen-king!" said Sue, and everybody laughed.

"Of course," Miss Nelson continued, "Traver felt very bad about losing the race. But what bothered him even more was that Fluff was made to suffer to keep him from winning the race. And yet, my brother never had an enemy in his life."

"What happened after that?" Pam asked.

"Well," the teacher said slowly, her face clouding over, "Traver and his dogs just—just disappeared into the forest. No one has seen or heard from him since."

"You mean," Sue said, "he's losted?"

"I'm afraid he is."

"Can't the Mounties find him?" Ricky asked hopefully, thinking of the fine work of the Canadian police.

Miss Nelson said the red-coated Mounties had been searching for her brother. But, although every so often they would find tracks in the snow they thought might be his, there had been no sign of Traver Nelson himself.

Holly ran over to the teacher. Looking up into her face, she said:

"Don't worry, Miss Nelson. Maybe your twin brother is training extra-special Eskimo dogs so he'll be sure to win the race this year."

Miss Nelson brightened at Holly's suggestion. "Maybe you're right, dear. If only Traver would send me word saying he's all right!" she said wistfully.

"I wonder"—Mrs. Hollister spoke up—"if those two men who came to visit you at school the day I substituted for you had anything to do with your brother's disappearance."

For a few moments, Miss Nelson did not reply. Finally she said thoughtfully:

"I hadn't thought of that, but they may have been responsible for Traver's going away. They came to my house and asked me if I knew where he is."

"Did they say why they wanted to know?" Pam asked.

"The men told me they wanted to buy Fluff," was Miss Nelson's startling answer.

"Buy Fluff?" Pam repeated.

The teacher nodded, adding that the men said they wanted to raise Eskimo puppies.

"They told me that since Fluff's feet had been injured, she would never be good for racing again."

"But that isn't true, is it?" cried Pam. "Fluff's feet may get better again."

"I can't answer that," Miss Nelson said.

Pete snapped his fingers. "Say! Maybe those men were the ones that took off Fluff's boots!"

"Yikes!" Ricky shouted. "I'll bet they did, so she'd get hurt."

"And your brother would have to sell her cheap!" Pete added.

Miss Nelson pondered this idea for a minute. "I never thought of that, but I'm inclined to believe you might be right."

"What are the men's names?" Mr. Hollister asked.

"They call themselves Mr. Gates and Mr. Stockman," the teacher replied.

"Do they live around here?" Pete wanted to know.

Miss Nelson was not sure, so the boy went to look in the telephone book.

Pete thumbed through the G's and the S's. There was one Miss Gates listed and a Paul Stockman.

"I'll call Miss Gates first," he decided. He dialed the number and spoke softly when the woman answered.

She said no Mr. Gates lived at that address and she had no relatives in Shoreham. Next, Pete phoned Mr. Stockman. From the sound of the man's voice, Pete was sure he must be pretty old. Mr. Stockman said he was definitely not the one the children sought.

"Well," said Pete as he sat down again at the table, "if those two men live in our town, they don't have a phone."

Pam thought it would be hopeless to find them this way. She had a more interesting idea.

"When we go to Canada, maybe we can hunt for your brother, Miss Nelson."

"That's a wonderful idea!" Holly exclaimed. "Then we can play we're Mounties!"

"Crickets!" said Pete eagerly. "We might even ride horseback on the search like they do!"

Hearing this really made Miss Nelson appear more cheerful.

"I understand you Happy Hollisters have solved mysteries before," she said. "If you should find my brother while you're in Canada, I could never thank you enough!"

As Mr. and Mrs. Hollister discussed their vacation plans with Miss Nelson, Ricky and Holly excused themselves and hurried upstairs. The others could hear a lot of giggling.

Mrs. Hollister glanced at the teacher. "They're up to something. We'll know in a minute."

Presently there was a clatter of feet on the stairway. Then Holly and Ricky raced into the dining room. Each wore a little red jacket, parts of clown costumes from the previous Halloween. On their heads were perched farmers' hats.

"We're Mounties! We're Mounties!" Ricky shouted.

He and Holly pretended to gallop across the room, and then disappeared into the kitchen.

"Now what are they up to?" Daddy Hollister chuckled.

All of a sudden there came a series of whispers and

"Mush! Mush!"

some meowing sounds. Then what a strange sight
emerged through the doorway!

White Nose, the cat, and her five kittens were harnessed together with twine. They scampered across
the floor, pulling a wicker market basket. Inside the
basket sat Holly's doll, Annie. Behind this contrap-
tion ran Ricky and Holly, yelling:

"Mush! Mush!"

Everyone burst out laughing. Round and round
the floor raced the cats. They turned a corner so fast
that the doll passenger went flying onto the rug.

"Help me, my brave Mounty," Holly called to
Ricky. "Please save my doll from the snowdrift!"

Ricky, the Canadian Mounted Policeman, got
down on his hands and knees, reached under the
chair, and pulled out Annie.

"See, she's not hurt at all!" he said proudly, setting the doll back in the basket dog sled.

By this time the cat and her kittens had become thoroughly tangled in their harness. They tumbled over and over, mewing and scratching at the string in their efforts to get loose.

"Let's free 'em. They can run back to the hills," Ricky said, and he and Holly untied the pets.

In a twinkling the six cats dashed back into the kitchen and curled up inside their own special box.

"If you all have half as much fun in Canada as you do right here," Miss Nelson said, "I know you'll have a wonderful visit."

In a little while the teacher said she must go. After Pam had brought her hat and coat, Miss Nelson thanked the Hollisters again and again for the lovely evening which she had enjoyed so much.

"And it was good to be able to talk to you about my brother. Somehow it's given me renewed hope!" she said.

The Hollister family assured the teacher they would try their hardest to locate him during their stay in Canada. As they walked with her to the front porch, Pete suggested that he and Pam accompany Miss Nelson home.

"That would be fine," she replied.

The children ran back for their coats and hats, then the three started off. Soon they were approaching the apartment house where Miss Nelson lived.

"Let's tell Officer Cal."

Suddenly Pete said, "Two men are standing across the street under that tree watching us."

"Miss Nelson, they look like the men who came to see you at school!" Pam added nervously.

As they were wondering what to do, the children saw Cal Newberry, a friendly policeman who had helped the Hollisters in earlier adventures, strolling down the street.

"I'll tell him," Pete offered.

"Pam and I will wait inside the apartment," Miss Nelson said.

Pete ran up to meet the policeman. "Officer Cal," he said in a low voice, "there are two suspicious men across the street. Their names are Gates and Stockman."

The policeman whirled in the direction the boy indicated.

No one was standing under the tree now!

87

CHAPTER 9

Blizzard!

"ARE you sure you saw two men you think are suspicious characters?" Officer Cal asked Pete Hollister.

"Oh yes," the boy insisted, and told the policeman the whole story.

"I'll look for them," Officer Cal said. "Can you describe the men?"

"Yes," Pete replied. "One's tall and heavy. The other's short and thin. Both of them are rough and mean-looking."

The policeman went off to try to find the men while Pete hurried into the apartment house. After he and Pam said good night to Miss Nelson, they hastened home, talking on the way about the mysterious men and why they wanted Fluff.

"Maybe she's a more valuable dog than anybody realizes," Pam remarked. "Oh, I hope Mr. Traver Nelson won't sell her to those awful people if they find him."

"Brrr!" Pete said, as he pulled the collar of his jacket up around his neck. "It sure is getting cold."

"Thanksgiving will be here before we know it," said Pam.

"It can't come too soon for me!" Pete exclaimed. "I want to get to Snowflake Camp as soon as possible."

The days flew by rapidly, and suddenly the Hollisters realized it was only a week before Thanksgiving. Late that afternoon it grew dark early and the air became very nippy.

"How about starting a fire in the fireplace, Dad?" Pete asked after the family had had supper.

"Fine," came the reply. "You and Ricky can be in charge."

"Come on, Ricky," Pete urged, hurrying out for some firewood.

His brother followed and they each brought in an armful of wood. Pete placed a few twigs in the fireplace and Ricky kindled a small blaze. As it crackled

Pete hurried out for firewood.

and popped, Pete put on more wood, and soon a merry fire was burning.

The Hollister children sat cross-legged on the hearth as close as they could get to the cheerful fire. Their mother sat in a chair on one side, mending, while Mr. Hollister reclined in his easy chair reading the evening paper.

"Let's shut off all the lights," Holly proposed. "May we, Mother and Dad?"

Mr. and Mrs. Hollister smiled. "Of course. I suppose you want to play the shadow game," Daddy Hollister said.

Pete sprang up and turned off the lamps. Now it was dark in the room except for firelight. And on the walls and floors were funny shadows of people and furniture. Some of them bobbed and danced.

"Watch my shadow do a jig, too," Sue piped up.

The little girl stood up and danced. Everyone laughed to see her shadow grow fat and skinny as it extended across the floor and then up the wall.

Each Hollister child took a turn. Pam could make shadow heads of donkeys and rabbits with her hands. Next Ricky got on Pete's back and they were a horse and cowboy.

Finally Holly stood with her feet apart, holding her pigtails straight out sideways from her head. She looked exactly like a scarecrow!

After their parents had applauded the impromptu show, Mrs. Hollister said, "How would you like to toast marshmallows over the embers?"

The marshmallows began to turn crispy brown.

Holly raced off for a big box of fat, white marshmallows. Pete, meanwhile, had hurried to the storeroom and returned with five long-handled forks.

Before anybody could say "marshmallow umbrella," five of the puffy candies were speared onto the forks and held over the embers by the children. In a few seconds they began to bubble and turn crispy brown. How good the living room smelled with the fragrant wood smoke and the sweetness of the cooking marshmallows!

When they were all eaten, Pete gathered up the forks. As he left the living room, he suddenly shouted:
"It's snowing!"

The other children dashed to the window. Large, white flakes were drifting to the ground.

"Oh, goody!" Holly said gleefully. "Now we can sleigh ride."

"And I can throw snowballs!" Ricky said. "And you know who I'm going to pop?"

"Not Joey Brill!" Pam teased.

"You guessed it," Ricky said.

"Better not go looking for trouble," Mr. Hollister warned his son.

"Oh, it's only make-believe," Ricky said. "I'm going to make a snow man and call him Joey and then knock his head off!"

The Hollisters laughed. As the children watched, the snowflakes became smaller and smaller and fell faster and faster.

"This looks like the beginning of a real blizzard," Mr. Hollister remarked. "If so, I'll need some helpers for shoveling in the morning."

Everyone offered to help. Then one by one the children went to bed.

Next morning it was strangely silent outside. Pete was the first to awaken. He jumped from bed and looked out the window. It was still snowing and drifts were four feet deep!

"Hey, wake up, everybody!" he shouted, running into the hall.

Soon everyone was awake. The children, excited, scurried about, dressed quickly, and raced to find their boots.

"Come on, we have to shovel the driveway so Dad can get the station wagon out," Pete reminded the others.

Pete was the first one to step out the back door.

The snow was up to the top step of the porch. He slipped from the edge of it and fell face down into the fluffy mass.

"Hurray, hurray, it's wonderful!" he said, getting up and plodding toward the garage.

"I wish I had some snowshoes," Ricky said, following him.

The boys found shovels for everyone, and they went to work quickly. Half an hour later Mrs. Hollister called them.

"Come get your breakfast. And hurry. There's a newscast on with an exciting report of storm conditions."

The children made their way to the back porch, where they stomped the snow off their feet and re-

He fell face down in the snow.

moved their boots. They had hardly entered their warm, cozy kitchen when they heard the broadcaster say:

"The storm is so severe that telephone lines are down in many parts of the county, making traveling dangerous. All schools in Shoreham will be closed until after Thanksgiving."

"Crickets! No school for ten days!" Pete shouted.

While Ricky and Holly skipped about happily, Pam stood thoughtful. Then suddenly her eyes brightened.

"Mother," she said, "if there's no school, we can go to Snowflake Camp earlier than we thought!"

Her father smiled. "That's a good idea." He looked at his wife. "You know, Elaine, there won't be too much business with traffic and transportation tied up. I can leave the store in Tinker's charge. Suppose we leave tonight if I can get train reservations."

What a shout of glee went up! After breakfast Mr. Hollister tried the telephone, but it was not working. He said he would have to go to the station to find out about tickets. Pleased to see the driveway was already cleared, the children's father immediately got out the station wagon.

"How about you boys going along and helping with the snow on the sidewalk at my store?" he asked.

His sons were keen to go. They never tired of the fascinating *Trading Post*. When they arrived, Tinker, a tall, elderly man who drove the store's delivery truck, was already shoveling snow in front of the place.

"Hi, Tinker!" Pete called, jumping out with his shovel.

" 'Mornin'," the man replied. "Two husky fellows to help me, eh? That's fine. This is the biggest snowstorm I've seen in many a year."

Pete and Ricky took opposite ends of the sidewalk and began to shovel. Every once in a while, Pete noticed his brother stoop for a few moments. When the walk was finally cleared, he said:

"Hey, Ricky, what were you bending over so much for?"

Ricky winked and beckoned to his brother.

"Come over here," he whispered.

Behind a telegraph pole was a stack of snowballs!

"I made them just in case——" he said, grinning.

Pete smiled, then he and his brother walked into *The Trading Post*. Their father was just coming back from the station.

"Any luck, Dad?" Pete asked.

"It's all set," he replied, his eyes twinkling. "I've made reservations for seven o'clock tonight."

Ricky gave a war whoop. "All aboard for Froston!" he shouted. "I'll go tell the others!"

"Just a minute, fellows," Mr. Hollister said. "I have something for you—a little reward for all that shoveling."

He handed each of the boys a pair of snowshoes.

"Yikes!" Ricky shouted. "Thanks, Dad!" Ricky threw his arms around his father and Pete slapped his dad on the back.

"We'll learn to use them pronto!" Pete said, and the brothers hurried out of the store. It did not take the boys long to strap on the snowshoes.

"These feel awful funny!" Ricky said, as he waddled along.

"There's a trick in using them," Pete replied. "Don't try to hurry too much, and lift your feet high."

The boys had gone only a block when they met Miss Nelson. Instantly they told her about their leaving on the night train for Snowflake Camp.

"How exciting!" she said.

"That'll give us more time to hunt for your brother," Ricky told her.

"Well, the best of luck," the teacher replied, as the boys started off.

Five minutes later they saw Officer Cal. He greeted them with a smile, saying the boys were certainly using their heads by traveling on snowshoes.

"That's what I should have," he laughed. "Guess I'll have to see your dad." Then he added seriously, "Those two men you wanted me to find have left town!"

"Where did they go?" Pete asked quickly.

"They left no address," the policeman said.

The boys were worried. Maybe the men had found out where Traver Nelson was!

As Pete and Ricky trudged home, their sisters, dressed in cute snowsuits with parka hoods, were coasting on a hill not far from their home. Pam was

"Giddap, Zip!"

pulling her own sled, while Sue and Holly shared a smaller one. Zip was bounding along beside them.

After a dozen rides Sue declared she was too weary to trudge back to the summit again.

"Suppose Zip pulls you up the hill," Pam suggested.

"Oh, let's try it," Sue urged.

Pam called Zip, who raced over to the girls. On the end of his nose was a big blob of snow.

"What have you been rooting for—rabbits?" Pam asked. "No more of that," she said, ruffling the collie's neck. "You have work to do."

Zip barked in agreement and stood still while Pam tied the sled rope to his harness. Then Sue got aboard and Pam said:

"Giddap, Zip!"

The dog started off, with Pam guiding him. When they reached the top, she untied the rope and hugged her pet.

"Good dog!" she said.

By this time a dozen other children had arrived and they all made a fuss over the collie.

"Let's go down once more," Holly begged, sitting on the sled in front of Sue and pushing with her feet in the snow to start them off.

Soon the sled was whizzing down the hill.

"Gangway!" Holly shouted gleefully as they passed first one sled, then another.

The two girls were nearing the bottom of the hill, going faster than ever, when suddenly a boy dashed out from behind a tree. As Zip bounded past him, the boy thrust out his foot and kicked the steering bar. The sled skidded around.

Head over heels went Holly and Sue, tumbling over and over in the snow!

CHAPTER 10

Snowshoe Detectives

FROM the top of the hill Pam saw her sisters fall off their sled. The boy who had caused the accident was Joey Brill!

Jumping on her sled, Pam raced down the slope. Stopping abruptly, she helped Holly pick herself up. The little girl's parka had fallen back and her eyes and ears were full of snow. Then Pam went to the assistance of Sue, who was coughing and choking from the snow in her nose and mouth.

"Oh, oh," she wailed, "my head hurts!" Sue had a red mark on her forehead.

Other children began to gather around the three girls. One of them was Donna Martin.

"Joey is the worst meany in town," she said. "If I were as big as he is, I'd wash his face in the snow!"

"The big coward ran away, too," declared another girl.

"Where did he go?" Pam asked.

"Down the road toward town."

"I wish Pete had been here," Pam said angrily as she brushed the snow off Sue. At least she would tell him about it.

At this very moment Pete and Ricky were approaching the hill on their snowshoes. Seeing them, Holly rushed over and quickly told the story of how Joey had dumped her and Sue into the snow.

"Oh, he did!" Pete said, clenching his fists. "He won't get away with this!"

"Picking on two little kids," Ricky put in. "Come on, Pete!"

The brothers headed back toward town, making good time over the snow. They had learned to use the snowshoes pretty well and no longer felt awkward lifting their feet high.

They saw Joey Brill in the distance and called to him. Joey looked at them over his shoulder but did not stop. Instead he started to run across a field.

"He's taking a short cut," Pete said, "but it won't do him much good. Snowshoes are better here than shoes."

The Hollister boys were amused to see Joey floundering in the snow as he tried to get away from them.

"He would have done better on the road," Ricky observed, matching strides with Pete.

The more Joey tried to hurry, the more he slipped in the deep snow.

"Go on! Go 'way from me!" he shouted, as Pete and Ricky gained on him.

"We will not," Ricky shouted. "We're going to wash your face for what you did to our sisters."

The thought of this spurred Joey on to greater speed. He finally came to the edge of the field and dashed to a road which had been partly cleared by snowplows.

Soon Joey was trotting down the street on which Mr. Hollister's store was located. Ricky and Pete kicked off their snowshoes, tucked them under their arms, and raced after the boy.

Joey flew past *The Trading Post*, but when Ricky arrived in front of it, the smaller boy stopped.

"Wait, Pete, grab these!"

He reached down behind the telegraph pole where the snowballs were concealed. Putting down their snowshoes, each boy picked up an armful of snowballs. Taking aim, they threw one after another at the fleeing Joey. One snowball hit him in the leg, another on the shoulder.

Pete took careful aim with his last bit of ammunition. *Whizzz!* The snowball knocked off Joey's cap. As he reached down to pick it up, Pete dashed across the sidewalk and tackled him. Over and over they rolled in the snow.

Although Joey was larger than Pete, the Hollister boy wrestled skillfully. Finally, Joey flopped over on his back with Pete kneeling above him.

"Hurray!" shouted Ricky.

Pete grabbed up a handful of snow and washed Joey's face.

"After this don't bother my sisters," he said, getting up.

Joey arose and did not fight any more. He shuffled

off down the street muttering defiance and threatening to get even at the first opportunity.

"You won't see us for a while," Ricky shouted after him. "We're going to Froston tonight."

Pete brushed himself off and the boys walked over to *The Trading Post*. Their father was just about to leave for home, and on the way he chuckled to hear of the face washing. They found Pam helping her mother with lunch. What a round of applause went up when the boys told what they had done to Joey Brill!

And how everybody cheered when Mr. Hollister said he had train reservations! The afternoon was a busy one, with children and parents packing. Sue tucked a doll into her little bag and Holly put a puzzle

"After this, don't bother my sisters."

in hers. Pam arranged for Tinker to feed Zip and White Nose and her kittens.

After an early supper Tinker came to drive the family to the railroad station. Sue was especially excited as they boarded the train.

"Good-by, good-by!" she called out, then said to Pam, "Are we really going to sleep in here?"

"Yes, honey," her sister replied.

"Does the train sleep, too?" Sue asked her.

Pam giggled and said that the train kept wide-awake so it would get the sleeping passengers where they wanted to go.

"Just like fairies would," Sue said. "But where are our beds?"

"It's magic," said Pam. "You'll see later."

Just before bedtime Mr. Hollister took his family to the buffet car for a little snack. When they returned to their seats, what a change had taken place! The seats had become beds!

"Oh, this is fun!" Holly exclaimed. "May I sleep in an upstairs bunk, Mother?"

Mrs. Hollister said she might. "And Pam will sleep with you. I suggest that Ricky and Pete take the one opposite you. The rest of us will take the lower berths."

A little later the porter came with a ladder, and all the children except Sue scrambled up.

Pam and Holly pulled their curtains shut and fastened them, but Holly kept giggling and whispering for a long time. Finally she popped her head out between the curtains and called to her brothers.

"What's up?" Ricky asked, unsnapping the curtains and poking his head out.

Then he laughed. Holly was holding her pigtails to look like a mustache. Slowly she reached out one hand with her fingers crooked like a witch's.

Ricky leaned forward to grab it. The next instant he lost his balance and started to tumble out of the berth!

"Oh!" cried Holly, trying to stop him.

Pete had seen his brother lean out too far and caught him by the leg. He held on until Mr. Hollister boosted the boy back up.

"Better not play any more games," their father advised.

Ricky leaned forward to grab her.

Soon the clickety-clack, clickety-clack, and the other wonderful noises that trains make at night put all the children to sleep. When Pete awakened in the morning, he was surprised to find Ricky gone. His clothes were there but not his robe and slippers.

"I guess Rick went to wash," Pete thought.

He put on his own robe and climbed down. But Ricky was not in the washroom at the end of the car, nor was he in sight. Seeing his father in the aisle, Pete asked him where Ricky was.

"I don't know," Mr. Hollister said. "He isn't with you?"

"No."

Mrs. Hollister, who was helping Sue in the berth with her, called out in alarm, "Where could he have gone?"

When they found out no one in the family knew where Ricky was, Mr. Hollister rang for the porter. He was a kind-looking man wearing a cap and a white jacket. They asked him if he had seen the little boy.

"No, sir," the porter replied with a worried look.

Other passengers were questioned. Not one of them had seen Ricky leave the car.

Sue clutched her mother's hand as the two left the berth.

"M—maybe Ricky fell off the train," she sobbed.

This remark startled everyone, but Mrs. Hollister said quickly, "I think my son has too much sense to do that." Then a sudden gleam came into her eye. "I think I know where he may be—in the kitchen."

"I'll find out," Pam offered, and hurried toward the dining car.

At the end of it she opened the door into the small kitchen. There stood Ricky Hollister in his robe, with a white apron tied around him and a chef's cap on his head.

"Hi!" he said to his sister, unaware that anyone had been worrying about him. "The chef let me help him make flapjacks!"

"You had us all frightened," Pam said. "Come on back."

Ricky took off his apron and cap. As he left, his new-found friend, the chef, winked at him. And later, when Ricky was having breakfast with his family, the waiter brought him an extra-tall stack of wheatcakes.

"The chef let me help him."

"This is from your friend, the chef," the waiter said, grinning.

The morning hours seemed to pass slowly for the children, who were eager to get to Froston. Pam made the acquaintance of a veterinarian in the car and listened to stories of his work.

Pete sat looking out the window thinking about the Trappers' Carnival and wondering if Fluff would race again this year.

"But maybe not if Mr. Gates and Mr. Stockman found Miss Nelson's brother and took the dog away!" he told himself.

The train now was running through a mountainous section with scattered pine trees. Pete held his cheek to the window trying to get a glimpse of the locomotive as it went around one bend after another.

Suddenly he saw something that horrified him. Without a moment's hesitation, the boy leaped up and pulled the emergency cord. With a grinding, jarring motion amid the shouts of passengers, the train came to an abrupt stop.

"What—what did you do that for?" Ricky shouted.

Pete pointed out the window.

CHAPTER 11

A Postman Named Stamp

THE door at the end of the sleeping car flew open. A conductor came running inside.

"Who pulled the emergency cord?" he demanded.

"I did," Pete Hollister replied, standing up. "I saw a doe and a fawn running onto the tracks. I was afraid they might be hit."

At first the trainman seemed annoyed, saying quick stops often injured people on a train, but then he added, "However, in this case——" and hurried off.

The Hollister children and their father quickly put on their coats, followed him outside, and walked down the track.

Pete had been right. On the track lay a small deer. The fawn apparently had hurt her right front leg while trying to cross the ties and was unable to use it. The doe was standing some distance away, anxiously looking on.

"Well, my boy," said the conductor, turning to Pete, "I'm glad now that you stopped the train. I certainly wouldn't want to hit a fawn." Then he added, "It looks as if her leg's broken."

While the others held the frightened fawn to keep

He put a splint on the fawn's leg.

her from trying to get away, Mr. Hollister bent down to feel the animal's foreleg. "I'm afraid it is broken," he said.

Pam started off. "I'll go get that nice vet I was talking to," she offered, and hurried back to the train.

In a few minutes he returned with her and put a splint and a bandage on the fawn's leg. Pete and Ricky lifted the animal to her feet. She looked up at them for a moment, then limped off toward her mother.

"The doe will help her baby take the bandage off at the proper time," the animal doctor said.

"Well," the conductor grinned, "we've delayed the train, but it was worth it."

"Yes," said Sue, "it made the mama deer very happy. We like to make people and animals happy.

That's why everybody calls us the Happy Hollisters."

The conductor and the veterinarian smiled as they all hurried back to the coach. Mrs. Hollister praised her son and other passengers came up to talk to the boy. Then everyone settled down once more as the train drew nearer and nearer Froston. Everything was covered with snow. Here and there a small town peeped out from the blanket of white.

Holly suddenly called out, "Oh, look, I spy a dog-sled team!"

Everybody glanced out the windows, including the porter. Far off in the distance on a little rise of ground was a fine-looking string of dogs. For a brief moment the animals were in sight. Then in a flurry of powdery snow, they pulled the sled into the woods.

"I wonder who the driver is." Ricky said.

The porter remarked that he was surprised to see anybody in these woods with a dog team.

"This is a rugged place," he said. "It's full of rocks that are covered by drifting snow. Few people from Froston ever come out this way with Huskies."

At once the Hollisters thought of the missing Traver Nelson. Could the driver possibly be the teacher's brother?

Ricky whispered to his Dad, "Do you suppose they'd stop the train while we followed the man a little way?"

"No, the train can't stop again," Mr. Hollister told his son. "It's late already and the engineer must make up time as it is."

Ricky was disappointed, but he and his brother and sisters became excited when their father added, "After we arrive in Froston we can come back this way and take a look."

A few hours later, the smiling conductor came into their car again. "Froston next stop," he announced.

The Hollisters eagerly arose from their seats and put on their coats and hats. The porter came to take their luggage off the train.

"Here's Froston!" Ricky shouted as he looked from the window.

First there was a white church steeple in the distance, then the little town came into view.

"Here's Froston!"

"It looks just like a picture-book village!" Pam exclaimed.

On either side of the tracks stood attractive small houses of many different colors. The red and green ones looked very pretty against the sparkling snow. Every street was decorated with lights and bunting.

"You'd think it was Christmas time!" Holly said.

The porter carried the bags down the steps and the Hollisters hastened to the wooden platform, where many people were waiting for guests.

Suddenly a deep, hearty voice called out from the edge of the platform, "Hello, there. Welcome to Froston!"

"Gramp!" Holly shrieked, jumping into the arms of a tall, ruddy-faced man with twinkling blue eyes.

"Gram!" Sue cried, hugging and kissing the sweet-faced, rosy-cheeked woman.

There were hugs and kisses and pats on the back as all the Hollisters greeted one another.

"Everyone ready for Snowflake Camp?" Gramp asked. When his son nodded, he said, "Come on, then. Gallant is waiting."

As they carried their baggage and the boys' snowshoes through the station, Pete asked, "Who's Gallant, Gramp?"

"Our new horse," his grandfather replied with a chuckle. "We didn't tell you about him. Wanted to keep it a secret."

On the far side of the station stood a red and white

"Yikes, a sleigh!"

sleigh. To it was harnessed a fine, big, dapple-gray horse.

"Gallant, meet our folks from Shoreham," Gramp said as Pam hurried over to pat the animal's nose.

"Yikes, a sleigh ride!" Ricky exclaimed as he helped his father stow the luggage in the sleigh. Then they all climbed in. The boys sat up front with the two men, while Gram and Mrs. Hollister squeezed into the rear with the three girls. Mrs. Hollister sat on the outside with Sue on her lap.

"May I drive, please, Gramp?" Ricky asked eagerly.

"Sure can," Gramp Hollister replied, "as soon as we get out of town."

Gramp drove them through the gaily decorated main street, then started for Snowflake Camp. At the edge of town he pointed out the various places where the winter sports of the Trappers' Carnival took place.

"The dog-sled race starts right here. And there's the ski jump." He pointed.

"Wow!" exclaimed Pete. "It's really high! Oh, look, a man's going to jump!"

The Hollisters held their breath as the skier flew through the air and landed smoothly on the snow below. Then Gramp showed them a special low ski jump for children.

"There's a girl coming down now," Gram called out. "That's Ruthie Jansen, the famous child skier. She's staying at our camp."

They all watched the graceful little girl make a perfect jump. She landed and coasted across the field toward the road. Gramp called to her.

"That was very pretty, Ruthie. I want you to meet my folks from the States," he added, introducing each one.

Ruthie replied in a delightful Norwegian accent, saying she was glad to meet them and would love to play with the children when she was not practicing.

"Are you going to be in a race?" Ricky asked her.

The child smiled. "It isn't exactly a race," she said. "It's a competition, though. You must come and see the children's jumping on Wednesday."

"We will," Pam promised, "and we'll see you at the camp."

Ruthie started back across the field and the Hollisters drove on. Gram explained that Ruthie was named for her English mother.

"Crickets, I wish we could compete in the Trappers' Carnival," Pete remarked.

"It sure would be neat," Ricky said. "Now may I drive, Gramp?"

As his grandfather handed him the reins, Ricky said, "Giddap, Gallant! Run!" The horse started at a fast clip and Sue clapped her hands gleefully.

As they neared a side road with a little house on the corner, the Hollisters heard a motor. Gazing to the right, they saw a vehicle that looked like a cross between a tractor and a sled. The front was supported by two skis, and the back by two rubber caterpillar tractors.

"Hello, Mr. Stamp!"

Gramp waved at the fur-capped man in the driver's seat. "Hello, Mr. Stamp!" he called out. When the driver stopped beside them, Gramp said, "Mr. Stamp, I'd like you to meet my son and his family."

Then he turned to the children and said, "This is our postman. Don't you think he's well named?"

The children smiled, then Ricky asked what he was driving.

"It's my snowmobile," Mr. Stamp said.

"A snowmobile!" Pete cried, hopping down off the sleigh to look at it. "Do you deliver mail in it?"

"Oh yes. Out here, where we have so much snow, mailmen and doctors use these snowmobiles to get around in. Would you children like to take a ride in mine?"

"Oh yes," they all cried.

When their parents gave permission, the other children got off the sleigh and all five climbed aboard the snowmobile.

"Meet you at the next crossroads," the postman called.

The rubber tractors went round and round and the skis glided smoothly over the snow.

"Crickets, this is really fast," Pete exclaimed, as they left the horse and sleigh far behind. "This would be good to use in searching through rough places for a missing person."

Mr. Stamp glanced at the boy.

"Do you have anybody in mind?" he asked.

"Yes. Traver Nelson," Pete replied. "Do you know him?"

"Yes, and I see you've heard he disappeared. Too bad. He was a fine fellow and had a splendid lead dog."

"You mean Fluff?" Pam asked.

"That's her name," the mailman answered. "Best Husky I've ever seen. Folks around here were hoping Traver would turn up for the Carnival and register his team for the race but he hasn't."

"Is it too late?" Pam asked quickly.

"No, but it will be by Wednesday night."

The children looked at one another, thinking how wonderful it would be if Traver Nelson and his dogs would come and race!

"You know," Mr. Stamp went on, "I believe Traver felt so bad about losing last year's race, he'll never sign up again. But he shouldn't feel that way. It's no disgrace not to win if you've done your best!"

"If we do find him," said Pam, "we'll tell him to register."

"Well, good luck," the man said. "And now here's the crossroads, where I must leave you. Nice meeting you young folks. I'll be seeing you again."

The children thanked him for the ride and when they saw the sleigh coming, got out. They waved good-by and he rode off just as Gramp reached them.

He said Pete might have a turn driving Gallant. As the boy guided the horse, *clippety-clop*, toward Snow-

"It's the strangest mystery we ever had."

flake Camp, Pam told her grandmother how they had found out about Traver Nelson.

"Mr. Stamp thinks he's too ashamed to come back," she said. "But I wish he would. My teacher, Miss Nelson, is very sad because she can't find her twin brother."

"It's the strangest mystery Froston ever had," Gramp remarked.

"We're going to try to find him," Pam announced.

"Well, you'll have to hurry if you expect to find him before those two men who are staying with us do."

"Gram, what do you mean?" Pam asked, puzzled.

As the children listened intently, their grandmother explained, "Two men who rented one of our cabins are looking for Traver Nelson right now."

CHAPTER 12

The Bear Scare

Two men looking for Traver Nelson! Could they be Stockman and Gates, Pam wondered.

Gram was quick to notice the girl's surprise. "Goodness gracious," she said, "you look as if you'd seen a snow fairy! What's so unusual about two men trying to find Mr. Nelson?"

Quickly Pam told her about the suspicious pair.

Gram adjusted her woolen scarf more snugly. "Well, stop worrying, dear. These men are brothers. And their name is Greeble."

Pam sighed in relief but Pete glanced at her as if to say he thought the men might be giving a false name.

"Let's go see them anyway as soon as we get to Snowflake Camp," he proposed.

"Are we almost there?" Sue asked impatiently.

"Just around the next bend," her grandfather replied.

Pete slapped the reins lightly on Gallant's back and the horse broke into a brisk trot.

"Here we are!" Gramp said, pointing.

A few feet ahead on the left side of the road was a

big sign pointing down a narrow lane. It said SNOW-FLAKE CAMP.

Pete guided the horse and sleigh along the tree-lined lane. Soon they came to a group of buildings scattered among tall trees. In the center stood a pretty gray cottage with red shutters. The others were log cabins. All were small except one, which was located a good distance from the cottage.

"Welcome to Snowflake Camp!" Gramp chuckled. "Pull right up in front of the cottage, Pete. That's where Gram and I live."

"Is ours the big house?" Sue asked.

"Yes, dear," Gram replied. "But first I want you all to come into the cottage and have lunch."

Leaving their baggage in the sleigh, the Hollister

"Welcome to Snowflake Camp!"

children followed their mother and father and grand-parents into the attractive three-room house. How cozy the living room was with its big fireplace and flowered curtains and bright-colored furniture covers! Beyond was a kitchen, and to the left a room with a four-poster bed.

"Oh, this is wonderful!" Pam spoke up.

As soon as lunch was over Gramp said, "I'll take you to your log cabin now."

Climbing into the sleigh once more, the Hollisters were driven toward their house. Pam asked where the Greeble brothers lived and Gramp pointed out their two-room cabin at the edge of the woods.

"The men told me they'd be gone all day," Gramp said.

The children helped carry the luggage inside their cabin and all Ricky had hoped for was true. The walls of the living room were decorated with fox skins and over the fireplace mantel hung a moose head with many-branched antlers. There was a large bear rug in the center of the room and comfortable couches and lounging chairs stood about in an attractive arrangement.

Gramp said, "Come, I'll show you and Pete where you're to sleep."

As he opened the door to a room off a little hall, Ricky jumped. A black bear stood there, its fore paws outstretched and its mouth opened angrily. The little boy fell back against his grandfather with a squeal of fright.

Ricky fell back with a squeal of fright.

Gramp and Pete laughed. Then suddenly Ricky realized that the animal was not alive. He was told it had been set in the room temporarily by the trapper who had captured it. The bear was to be moved to town that afternoon.

Ricky's eyes lighted up. "Please, may I scare the girls before you take it away?"

When Gramp nodded yes, Ricky closed the door and ran off for his sisters. Two minutes later there were shrieks and screams as he showed them the live-looking bear.

After the excitement died down, the Hollisters unpacked. Then the children pushed the bear into the living room and played hunting and trapping for a while. Sue and Holly were helping Ricky round up their "catch" when there was a knock on the door.

"I'll go," Pete offered.

When he opened it, he saw a boy only a little older than himself standing there, a large sled behind him. The dark-eyed youth smiled and said he had been sent to pick up the bear by its owner. Pete invited him in, saying he would help the boy.

"My name's Pierre," said the newcomer, addressing all the children. "I do errands for your grandfather. You've just arrived, haven't you?"

"Yes," Pete replied. "Do you work here all the time?"

"Oh no. Just after school. Say," he added, "maybe you'd like to come and visit our school. It's probably pretty different up here from the one you go to."

All the children said they would like to attend and Pierre suggested that Monday would be a good time. Then quickly the Hollisters put on their snowsuits and helped Pierre load the bear onto his sled. They steadied the animal as he pulled the sled down the narrow lane to the road. There a large sleigh was waiting to carry the bear away.

As the children walked back, Ricky asked Pierre if he had any animals. The Canadian boy laughed.

"Yes, I have a raccoon and a beaver. But better than that, I have two Huskies."

"Yikes! Can I see them?" Ricky asked.

"Sure. I'll take you to my house sometime."

Pierre said he must gather firewood, and at once the Hollisters offered to help. When the job was finished, Pierre thanked them and said good-by.

Dusk was coming on and lamps had been lighted in several of the cabins. Suddenly Pete exclaimed:

"Look! The Greeble brothers are home!"

"Let's go find out right away if they're the ones we saw in Shoreham," Pam proposed.

Pete led the way, followed by Holly and Ricky. Pam brought up the rear.

Pete knocked boldly on the door. The children waited for a reply, but no one answered.

"Knock again," Pam urged.

Rap, rap! Pete knocked harder. There was silence for a moment, then a deep, gruff voice shouted:

"Go away!"

The command startled the children.

"Do you think we'd better go?" Holly asked, a little frightened.

Pete knocked boldly on the door.

Her brother's answer was another knock on the door.

"We want to speak to you, please," he called out.

Suddenly a crack of light showed as the door opened an inch. Then as it opened wider, the children saw two men, wearing heavy black beards, standing in the doorway. They could not be Stockman and Gates! Both men had been clean-shaven in Shoreham!

"I—excuse us, we—uh, thought we knew you," Pete apologized.

The men said nothing; merely stared at the children. Then Ricky spoke up. "Why are you looking for Mr. Traver Nelson?"

The men seemed startled by the question. Then the shorter of the two said gruffly:

"Because his sister wants us to find him."

Pam was amazed. Miss Nelson had not told them that she had asked anybody to trail her brother.

In the awkward silence that followed, the children did not know what to say. Finally Pete managed:

"Well, thank you very much."

The Hollisters went home but continued to wonder about the men. Pete and Pam thought they had acted very unfriendly. Why?

"If they should be Mr. Stockman and Mr. Gates," said Pam, "they probably recognized us."

"Let's trail them tomorrow," Pete suggested.

Next day being Sunday, the Hollisters went to church with Gram and Gramp. After returning, Pete

The children started downhill.

learned from a neighbor that the Greebles had left their cabin early.

"Never mind," said Pam. "If they find Mr. Nelson, we'll hear about it soon."

But Pete wanted to make a search himself for Mr. Nelson and spoke to his father about going with him.

"Can't we go to the place where we saw the dog team from the train?" he begged.

Mr. Hollister spoke to Gramp, who was enthusiastic but said the only way to get there was by snowmobile.

"I'll phone Mr. Stamp," he said.

Fortunately, he found the postman at home. He would be glad to lend the snowmobile and would pick up Pete and his father in an hour.

In the meantime the other children made plans to have Ruthie Jansen teach them something about skiing. Carrying skis and poles which Gramp lent them, the four Hollisters followed Ruthie to a gently sloping hill. After everyone was ready, the Norwegian girl gave them some pointers on how to bend their bodies and dig in the poles. Then the children started downhill.

Plop!

Pam and Ricky fell almost at the same time. Sue, who was using small skis, lost her balance an instant later. The three sat laughing in the snow, then struggled to their feet.

Holly, however, had reached the bottom of the hill without a spill. Ruthie applauded her, saying, "That was wonderful, Holly!"

Everyone agreed, as the practice went on, that the pig-tailed girl was the best ski pupil. But the other Hollisters, although they tried and tried, rarely got all the way down without falling.

"Gee, I'm starting to ache," said Ricky, grinning.

Pam and Sue admitted they were a bit sore too, but Holly declared she could go on skiing all afternoon. Ruthie smiled and promised her another lesson soon.

"I must go now and practice for the race," she said.

Before Ruthie left, Pam asked her if she had taken part in the Trappers' Carnival the year before.

"No, I was home in Norway," she replied.

Pam told her about the missing Mr. Nelson and his lovely lead dog, Fluff.

"Did you say Fluff?" Ruthie asked excitedly.

When Pam nodded, Ruthie said that two days before, while she was practicing on the ski jump, she had walked back up the hill through the woods.

"I heard two men talking," she half whispered. "One of them told the other, 'Nothing's going to stop me from getting Fluff!' "

"Oh!" Pam exclaimed. "What did the men look like?"

Ruthie told her she had not seen them. She was sorry. Pam was sorry too. But at least it proved one thing: Two men definitely were trying to steal the beautiful Eskimo dog!

That evening when Pete and his father returned, Pam ran to tell them her news. Pete whistled. This was a good clue!

"Dad and I didn't learn a thing," he reported in disgust. "I'm afraid Mr. Nelson may be nearer

"Gee, I'm starting to ache," said Ricky.

Froston than we think and walking right into a trap if he comes here."

The boy decided to do more sleuthing. One thing would be to spy on the two suspicious men at Snowflake Camp. Directly after supper he took a flashlight and set off in the darkness for their cabin.

"I mustn't get caught," he told himself.

Hiding behind a tree, the boy watched the bearded men moving about in the house. When Pete saw his chance, he came closer, then dashed behind another tree. Just then the door of the cabin was flung open.

"I thought I heard somebody out here, Stocky," the taller of the men cried in a rough voice. "Bring a flashlight!"

Stocky! Could this mean Stockman?

Pete decided to find better cover. Spying a woodpile a few feet away, he made a dash for it. Some of the logs had been removed from the center of the pile. Pete wriggled into this spot and quickly brushed some snow on top of himself. He was not a moment too soon.

"Where did you say you saw him?" Stocky growled.

"Over there behind the tree."

Through a crack in the woodpile, Pete could see the beam of a flashlight flicking back and forth among the trees. He held his breath as it came closer and closer to the woodpile.

CHAPTER 13

Fire !

"Hmmm. What did I tell you?" the man cried. "The tracks lead right to this here woodpile."

He laid one hand on a log just inches above Pete's head, but the snow camouflaged the boy so well that in the darkness the man missed seeing him.

"I suppose it was one of those Hollister kids and we scared him away," Stocky said. "Let's get back inside before we freeze." He laughed. "It'd be too bad to get sick and not be able to find Traver Nelson by the time that race starts."

Pete pricked up his ears. Why was it so important for these men to find their teacher's twin brother before the big race started? He hoped the men would reveal more, but both remained silent as they entered the cabin and slammed the door.

Pete carefully wriggled out of the woodpile and headed for home. Suddenly a new thought about the Greeble brothers came to him.

"I wonder if they could be policemen!" the boy said to himself. "Maybe Traver Nelson did something wrong."

Arriving at the Hollisters' log cabin, Pete told the

others what he had overheard and his new theory about them. Pam quickly sprang to the defense of her teacher's twin.

"I'm sure he didn't do anything wrong," she insisted. "Miss Nelson said that her brother was very sensitive. He ran away because of the bad men who made him lose the race."

Mr. Hollister laid a hand on his daughter's arm and said, "What Pete says might be true. And I advise you children to have a good time and stop worrying about the Greeble brothers. I learned from Gramp today that they came here with very high recommendations."

Pete looked at his sister, then shifted his glance to his dad. Which one was right? Pam's trust in people was usually well founded. Besides, Mr. Stamp had said Traver Nelson was a fine person. Pete hoped that this was the case and that the Greebles were not policemen.

Next morning the children dressed for their visit to the Canadian country school. At eight o'clock Gramp Hollister drove up in the sleigh. In it were three pairs of snowshoes. Gramp told Pete and Ricky to bring theirs.

"This is the way youngsters up here go to school in the wintertime," he said.

When they were ready to leave, the children waved to their parents and off they drove. The bells on Gallant's harness jingled merrily. In a few moments they were in front of the school, a small white building that

"We were expecting you," said the teacher.

looked something like a little church without a steeple. A young woman stood in the doorway swinging a large bell in her hand. Pupils, climbing the steps, stopped to kick the snow off their boots and remove their hats before they entered.

The Hollisters heard one little boy about Ricky's age remark, "I say, what a big family of kids that's moved to Froston!"

Ricky grinned at him. "We're just visitors," he said, "from the United States."

"We were expecting you," said the young woman, smiling. "Pierre phoned me. He'll be a little late. I'm Miss Johnson. Will you follow me?"

She requested them to put their coats, caps, and snowshoes on hooks just inside the door.

Following her inside, the Hollisters found that

there was only one classroom, heated by a little round coal stove which stood near the back on the left. The desks were of various sizes for the different age groups.

When Miss Johnson reached the front of the room, she turned to the pupils and introduced the visitors, asking each one to give his first name. Then she said:

"Please make yourselves at home and sit wherever you like."

Pete and Pam seated themselves with some of the older children while Holly, Ricky, and Sue found places with the younger pupils. The morning session began. First Miss Johnson would teach one group of children while the others worked quietly. Then she would leave them and go on to the next grade.

Presently she told the Hollisters this was the day of the week when the older children studied United States history and affairs. Perhaps the visitors would like to take over.

"Oh, I know a lot about our country!" Ricky exclaimed proudly.

Miss Johnson smiled. "Suppose you tell us about your own state, then," she said.

Ricky did the best he could, saying it had lots of factories that made just about everything, then Pete and Pam added more information. Miss Johnson next asked Holly to tell about Lincoln School activities. The little girl mentioned the various clubs and said Pam was president of the Pet Club.

"That's how we found out Pam's teacher is the

sister of Mr. Nelson who lost the race last year," she said.

The pupils were amazed to hear this. All of them knew about Fluff and hoped to see the lovely dog race again this year. None of them could offer any suggestion as to where the man and his Eskimo dogs might be.

"And now," said Miss Johnson, turning to Sue, "what can you tell us about the place you live in?"

Sue had been sitting quietly making pictures with the youngest group.

"We have lots of snow too," the little girl replied. "There was a big bliz."

"She means blizzard," Pam said, and the children laughed.

"Anyhow," Sue went on, "nobody could go to school so we came up here to eat turkey with my grandmother."

This remark led to a talk by Miss Johnson about Thanksgiving, which is not celebrated in Canada. When she mentioned the good things usually eaten with the turkey, Pierre, who had come in a few minutes before, declared it made him very hungry.

At recess all the children except Sue, who decided to stay in and draw, put on their caps and snowsuits. One of the older boys tossed a couple of logs into the stove and the pupils dashed outside to play, followed by the teacher.

A few minutes later Sue raced out the door, calling:

Miss Johnson was trying to beat out the fire.

"Ricky! Pete! Come here quick! The stove's making a fire!"

At first her brothers thought Sue was fooling, but when they noticed a look of alarm on her face, they rushed back into the classroom. The top of a desk was in flames! Papers on it had been ignited by sparks flying through the open door of the stove.

Without hesitation, Pete slammed the door shut, then the Hollister brothers dashed outdoors and grabbed up handfuls of snow. By this time Miss Johnson had run in and was trying to beat out the flames with a shovel. Between this and the snow the fire was soon extinguished.

John, the boy who had put the logs in the stove, was aghast. He had closed the door but evidently not tightly enough and it had swung open.

Miss Johnson advised him to be more careful in the future and praised the Hollisters for their quick wits. "We're lucky to have had you visit us today," she said. "If it hadn't been for Sue and you boys there might have been a bad fire in the school."

At lunch time the Hollisters said good-by to Miss Johnson and all the pupils. Since they planned to walk back to Snowflake Camp on snowshoes, they took a short cut which Pierre pointed out. It took them through a lane to a side road.

They had not gone far on this road when Ricky spied an old deserted farmhouse ahead. Always looking for adventure, the boy trudged into the grounds and opened the door of an abandoned barn behind the main building.

"Hey kids, come here quick!" he shouted. "See what I found!"

His brother and sisters raced over. Ricky pointed to a pile of straw on the floor. Lying in the middle of it was an Eskimo-dog puppy.

"Oh, how adorable!" Pam cried, reaching down to stroke its fluffy fur.

The other children got down on their haunches, surrounding the beautiful buff puppy. Holly reached out her hand to pet him.

"Oh dear, I'm afraid the poor little thing will catch cold," she said tenderly.

Pam chuckled when she heard this. "I don't think so. Eskimo dogs can stand very low temperatures," she replied.

"Let's take him home," Ricky proposed.

"Oh no," Pam said. "I'm sure his mother will return for him."

On the way to their cabin, Ricky kept talking about the puppy, and late that afternoon his curiosity to see if the dog was still there got the better of him.

"Pam," he said, "please come back with me and look at him."

"All right, I will," his sister agreed. "But don't forget—we're not bringing him home."

Ricky grinned but said nothing. The other children joined him and Pam in their trek back to the barn. It was not far from Snowflake Camp. As they approached the door, Ricky said:

"Listen! Hear that whining? The mother didn't come back for her puppy after all."

He slid the barn door open and stared in amaze-

"Yikes! Now there are two of them."

ment. Then the boy shouted, "Yikes! Now there are two of them!"

"But how did this one get here?" Holly cried.

Pete grinned. "If his mother didn't bring him, then it's another mystery we'll have to solve."

As Pam stroked the puppies, she said no doubt they were from the same litter. She lifted them off their straw bed and the younger children watched as the puppies waddled about.

Meanwhile, Pete looked around for dog tracks to see where the mother had gone but could find none in front of the barn. In the rear, however, he could see prints coming and going through a hole between two clapboards. He followed the footprints for a distance, but they became lost where the wind had scattered the snow around. The boy turned back and joined his brother and sisters.

"Let's stop at Gram and Gramp's and tell them about the pups," he proposed. "Maybe they know where the dogs came from."

But both grandparents said they knew nothing about them.

"Why do you suppose the mother dog left them in the barn?" Pam asked.

"There might be danger where the pups were living," Gram replied. "Dogs always see to it that their puppies are safe."

Pam said that she was going to visit the barn first thing in the morning to see if the mother dog was there. Then maybe she would lead the girl to her old

"Look at this, Pete!"

home and Pam could find out what had happened.

"Maybe Pierre knows about them," Holly suggested.

The boy was still working at the camp and the children hurried off to ask him. But Pierre had not heard of any dog in the neighborhood who had had pups recently.

Next morning Pete and Pam were up early and met in the kitchen. Their mother gave permission for them to visit the barn and they set off at once toward the abandoned farmhouse.

Approaching the barn, they heard the whining of pups. This time it seemed to be louder. Pete opened the door and Pam peered inside. "Look at this, Pete!" she exclaimed.

Instead of two puppies, now there were three!

CHAPTER 14

Tracking a Husky

PETE and Pam bent down to pick up the three puppies.

"Oh, you poor things," the girl said as she cuddled them. "You look hungry."

"They need some raw, fatty meat," Pete observed. "Remember, we learned that when we were studying about Eskimo dogs."

The children were tempted to take the puppies home to feed them, but decided to bring the food to the barn instead.

"We'll hurry right back after breakfast," Pete said.

"Look, they don't want us to leave," Pam remarked as the fuzzy little animals nuzzled close to her.

She laid the puppies back in the straw and piled some of it around them to keep the animals cozy. Then she and Pete hurried back to the cabin. Mrs. Hollister had prepared a hearty breakfast of bacon, eggs, and toast for them, and as they ate, the older children told about the discovery of the third puppy.

Ricky grinned. "Yikes!" he exclaimed. "If we wait

long enough, maybe the whole barn will be full of Eskimo dogs!"

After breakfast Pam asked for meat to give the pups. Her mother smiled.

"You'll find a fatty piece of beef in the refrigerator, dear. Take that."

As the children trudged up to the old barn, Holly asked, "What color is the new puppy?"

"Gray," Pam told her, as Pete opened the door.

Suddenly Ricky said, "Good joke! We fell for it! Three pups, eh? There are still only two."

Pete and Pam stared at each other, saying this was no joke. There had been three! Quickly they searched the barn, but the third puppy was not in it. All the children looked around outside. The little Eskimo dog had vanished!

"But why," said Sue, "would his mommy bring him here and take him right away again?"

Pete frowned. "I just hope nobody stole the dog," he said.

"Stole him!" the others exclaimed, and Pam added, "Maybe we ought to guard the barn!"

"That's a good idea," Pete agreed. "Let's talk to Dad about it."

Pam gave the puppies the meat she had brought, then the children hurried back home. Gram was at the cabin, saying she thought it strange that the Greeble brothers had been away from their cabin since Sunday evening.

"They may have had to go a long way in their

search for Mr. Traver Nelson," Mrs. Hollister remarked.

"No doubt," Gram said.

The older Hollisters were very interested in the story of what Sue called the "coming-and-going" pup and Mr. Hollister offered to stand guard during the morning.

"Suppose Holly and Sue come with me," he suggested. "While we're watching the barn, we'll make a big snowman."

By twelve o'clock they had built a tall, fine-looking figure that gleamed in the sun.

All this time there had been no sign of a visitor to the barn. Mr. Hollister said that he and his daughters should return to the cabin now. It was lunch time. When they arived, Pete said:

"Pam and I will take the afternoon shift."

They built a tall, fine-looking figure.

How hungry everyone was! Each member of the Hollister family ate two helpings of the delicious chicken fricassee and apple pie.

Ricky was the first to finish and asked to be excused. He put on his jacket and boots and hurried outside. While Pam and Holly were helping their mother wash the dishes, they heard a noise under the floor. Then came a muffled shout from Ricky.

"It sounds as if Ricky found something in the cellar," Mrs. Hollister smiled.

The family soon learned what it was. Ricky burst into the kitchen breathlessly.

"Guess what!" he cried out. "There's an old dog sled in the storage cellar. Come on, Pete, help me pull it out."

"I think you'd better ask Gramp about that first," Mrs. Hollister advised. "Maybe he's keeping it there for a special reason."

Ricky dashed out the door and raced to his grandfather's cottage. In a few minutes he was back again, more out of breath than he had been before.

"Gramp," the boy gulped excitedly, "said we could take the dog sled out. It's a komatik, like you hitch Huskies to."

"I wonder where he got it?" Pam asked.

"From an old trapper," Ricky replied. "Gramp said he put it away and forgot he had it."

All the Hollisters hurried outside and Ricky led them to the door in the side of the house which

"Let's make believe we're Eskimos."

opened into the storage bin. He and Pete dragged the komatik out.

"Isn't this swell?" Ricky cried.

"It's wonderful!" Pam exclaimed.

A harness was attached to it, and as Pete examined the thongs he remarked, "Do you remember, Pam? This is called a gang hitch. We saw pictures of it in the school library books."

"Let's make believe we're Eskimos and take a ride," Holly said, jumping onto the sled.

"All right," Pete agreed. "Ricky and I will pull you girls."

This proved to be hard work, and presently they stopped. Ricky said, "Say, Pierre has two Eskimo dogs. Maybe he'd let us hook them up to this komatik and pull us around."

The others thought this would be fun and decided

to ask the boy when he came to work. As if in answer to their wish they suddenly saw Pierre coming through the woods and ran to meet him. He explained that school had closed early because of trouble with the stove.

"That's good," said Ricky, not realizing how this sounded. "Pierre, could we borrow your dogs to pull our komatik?"

The Canadian boy smiled. "Indeed, yes. My Huskies used to work in a dog team. They'll know just what to do."

Pete and Ricky went with him to get the dogs. When they returned all the children talked to the handsome animals and petted them. Pierre harnessed the dogs, then said:

"All aboard! Who wants to ride first?"

It was decided that Pierre would drive the dogs and give Sue a turn first. The little girl giggled and screamed in glee, "I'm a Eskimo girl!" as the komatik went in a circle around the Hollister cabin.

Then Holly took a ride and Ricky was next. As Pierre brought the dog sled to a halt, he said:

"Pete, how about you driving? Give Pam a ride."

Grinning, Pete stepped onto the back of the komatik. Pam seated herself, then suggested they ride to the barn. She explained about the missing pup to Pierre and said she and Pete were going to watch the place.

Pierre said he would follow and bring the dogs

back. "This certainly is a mystery," he remarked. "I hope you solve it this afternoon."

Pete called out to the Huskies, "*Mush!*" and away they started. Upon reaching the barn, he said to his sister:

"Boy, this was great. I'd like to drive a team in a dog-sled race someday."

Pam smiled at her brother as she got off the komatik. In a few moments the others arrived and Pete slid open the barn door.

A gasp came from the children. There was only one puppy left!

Pam looked fearfully at Pete, "We shouldn't have left this place unguarded a moment!"

Sue began to cry. "The poor doggie's been stole by the bad men!"

Away the dogs went!

Pierre looked puzzled, so Pete told him the story of Stockman and Gates. He added that the children were suspicious that the Greeble brothers might be the "bad men" in disguise. One had the nickname of Stocky.

The older boy whistled in amazement. As he and the younger children got ready to go back to camp, Sue grabbed Pam's hand.

"Don't let the bad men get you," she begged.

"We won't," her sister promised. "Pete and I will come and get Dad and Gramp."

Sue felt better and seated herself on the komatik for the ride back. After Pete and Pam had been left alone, they walked around to see if they could figure out who had been there.

"No footprints," Pete said at last.

A little later in the afternoon, Pam said she thought they ought to leave. At this moment the children were standing near the snow man behind the barn.

Pete grabbed his sister's arm. "Look!" he whispered. "A dog!"

A beautiful buff-colored Eskimo dog with a deep chest and large, fluffy tail was making her way to the barn. As the brother and sister looked on excitedly, the dog went through the opening between the clapboards and disappeared inside. A moment later she emerged with the puppy held firmly in her teeth.

"Oh, I'm so happy she came after her puppy," Pam said. "Let's go speak to her."

Pete held his sister back. "She might be the famous

The Husky emerged with the puppy.

Fluff," he said excitedly. "She looks like the one we saw on TV."

"Yes, she does," Pam agreed.

"Suppose we follow her," Pete proposed. "She might lead us to Traver Nelson!"

Hopefully the children dashed after the Husky, keeping far enough behind so she would not become suspicious. Her tracks were easy to follow whenever they lost sight of her. They hurried along for nearly fifteen minutes, then the dog led the way down through a little gully filled with snow and big boulders. The animal suddenly vanished.

"How are we going to get around this big rock?" Pam asked.

Pete put out his hand to touch the huge rock. A startled look came over his face.

"Pam!" he whispered hoarsely. "This isn't a rock. It's the wall of a cabin!"

His sister stared in amazement. Then she noticed a place where the snow seemed to glow a short distance away. Her heart pounding, she stepped closer to it and beckoned to her brother.

"Pete," she said in a low voice, "this is a window that's covered with snow!"

For a moment the two children conversed in whispers. Should they try to find the dog, or should they look inside the strange, camouflaged cabin?

"Let's peek in," Pete suggested.

Pam put her mitten to the window and brushed away some snow. The children peered inside. They gasped fearfully at what they saw.

They gasped fearfully at what they saw.

149

CHAPTER 15

Wonderful News

LOOKING into the cabin, Pete and Pam could make out a small, flickering fire in a corner fireplace. On a cot in front of it was a thin-faced man and standing beside him were two bearded woodsmen.

"The Greeble brothers!" Pete whispered.

As the three men talked, their voices began to rise. The one nicknamed Stocky shook a finger at the man who was lying down.

"Listen here, Nelson!" he said. "We want that dog. Where is she hiding?"

At the name Nelson, both children gave a start.

"Traver Nelson!" Pam said, shaking with excitement. "We've found him!"

"Sh! sh!" Pete warned. "Listen to what they're saying."

When Mr. Nelson did not reply, the other brother said, "We'll find Fluff and her pups, so you might as well tell us. Where is she?"

Traver Nelson mumbled a reply which the children could not hear. The Greebles looked disgusted and tramped toward the door on the far side of the room.

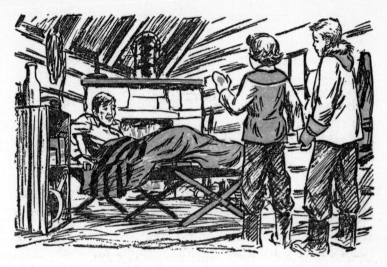

"Don't be frightened, we've come to help."

Pete and Pam ducked out of sight and quickly discussed what to do. They could not hope to capture the men.

"But," Pete vowed, "if they try to take Fluff and and the pups, I'll stop them!"

"Oh, I hope she's well hidden and won't give herself away!" Pam cried.

Both children held their breath. There was not a sound from Fluff as the two men slammed the door and stalked off. In a few minutes they disappeared from view.

"Maybe we ought to go home and tell the police," Pete urged. "Come on!"

But Pam, who had turned to look in the window once more, said, "No, Pete. Poor Mr. Nelson seems to be ill. We must see if we can help him."

Pete led the way around the corner of the building to the door.

"It's well hidden," he said, hunting for the latch.

When the children stepped inside the almost bare shack, the man looked frightened for a moment. He struggled to sit up on the cot, feebly supporting himself on his elbows.

"Don't be frightened," Pam said. "We're the Happy Hollisters and we've come to help you."

"And you're Traver Nelson, aren't you?" Pete said, looking directly into the man's eyes.

At this the man sank back onto the cot and asked in a strained, husky voice, "The Happy Hollisters? You've come to help me? How did you know——?"

"Your sister is Pam's teacher," Pete said. "She wants desperately to find you. Miss Nelson hasn't heard from you for a year."

Traver Nelson reached out a hand and rested it on Pam's arm. "You mean she never received my letters? That's too bad. When I decided to go far away and not return until just before the race, I wrote her that. I guess the man I gave the letters to never mailed them."

Traver Nelson said he had arrived three days before and had been ill ever since. His food supply and the dogs' meat was gone.

"Three days ago!" Ricky exclaimed. "Say, were you driving your team near the railroad last Saturday morning?"

"Yes."

"Where are your dogs?" Pam asked.

"Two wicked men have stolen all but one since I got here. She's my lead dog, Fluff. Last year they tried to buy her cheap when she didn't win the race. Since I wouldn't sell, they attempted to steal her. That's why I hid."

Pam told him about finding Fluff's puppies in the deserted barn and Mr. Nelson managed a little smile.

"Fluff is very smart," he said. "To fool those men, I told Fluff to take her pups away and she did."

"But she has brought them back again," Pam said, worried. "We must get them away before those men return."

Mr. Nelson explained that the children would find the dogs in a secret, snow-covered kennel which could be entered only through an opening in the

"We must get Fluff out!"

rocks. He told Pete how to find it and pointed to a flashlight on the mantel shelf.

Pete took it and went outdoors. When he found the kennel, the boy leaned down, beamed the flashlight into the opening, and called:

"Fluff! Come here, Fluff!"

At first there was no reply, but finally the fine head of the Eskimo dog appeared at the opening.

"Your master wants you," Pete said, patting the Husky. "And your puppies, too."

The mother dog turned back into the kennel. A moment later, she returned carrying the gray pup. Pete held it while she went for the other two.

Pete took them all into the cabin again. Fluff bounded over to Traver Nelson and licked his hand. The puppies nestled down before the fire.

"What are their names?" Pam asked.

"The buff one is Taffy, the white one, Arctic, and the gray one, Dawn," the man replied. He looked fondly at Fluff. "Old girl, my dream about the race is gone. You and I won't win it this year either. And the Mounties won't know how good your pups are, so they won't buy them."

Pete tried to console the man. "Couldn't you get another team for Fluff and have somebody else drive them?" he suggested.

"No, I don't think Fluff would work for anybody else," Mr. Nelson replied.

Pam had gone to look out the window and said it

was getting late. She and Pete ought to leave at once before it grew dark in the woods.

At this moment the children were suddenly startled to hear their names called. Pam rushed outside and around the shack, followed by Pete. At the top of the gully stood Holly with Ruthie Jansen! Both were on skis.

"Oh, I'm glad we found you!" Holly cried in relief. "Mother sent us to look for you at the barn and you weren't there!"

"We followed your footprints," Ruthie said.

Quickly Pete explained what had happened. Then he said, "On skis you can get back to the camp much faster than we can on foot. Hurry, and ask Mother to phone for a doctor."

"Hurry, and bring help!"

"And tell her Pete and I will come with Fluff and the pups," Pam added.

The two young skiers excitedly glided away. Pete and Pam rushed back into the cabin to inform Mr. Nelson that medical help would soon come to him and that they would take the Huskies home.

"We'll guard the dogs well so the Greebles can't get them," Pete promised.

"You're wonderful children," the sick man said. He turned to Fluff. "Go with them," he directed.

When the children and the dogs reached the Hollisters' cabin, the excitement was intense. The whole family was there. Pete and Pam received plenty of praise. Gramp rushed over and put his arms around them.

"You children have done what nobody else could!" he cried. "You actually found Traver Nelson!"

Gram explained that they had telephoned a doctor in town. He would be out immediately.

"And what's more"—Ricky spoke up—"Mr. Stamp's bringing him in his snowmobile. And they're going to get Mr. Nelson in it and drive him here."

"I can play nurse," said Holly, "and help him get better."

"Mother," said Pam, "don't you think we should notify Miss Nelson right away?"

Mrs. Hollister nodded. "Go to Gramp's cabin and phone the telegraph office," she suggested.

The doctor trudged toward the door.

"And I'll walk over with you"—Mr. Hollister spoke up—"and notify the Mounties about the Greebles."

Just as they finished telephoning and sending the wire to Miss Nelson, the snowmobile drove in to Snowflake Camp. Pam and her father followed it to their cabin. Mr. Stamp and a young man jumped out.

"So you've found Traver Nelson!" Mr. Stamp said as the family crowded around, and he introduced his companion as Dr. Jacques. "Where is he? We'll go for him immediately."

"We'll show you," Pete offered, and he and Pam climbed aboard. On the way the children told Mr. Stamp and the doctor the full story and both men said they would like to help capture the Greebles.

With Pete and Pam directing, it did not take the snowmobile long to reach the well-hidden shack.

"I never could have found this myself," the doctor remarked.

Pete and Pam waited outside with Mr. Stamp. In a few moments the physician called them to come in.

"Mr. Nelson's poor condition is due entirely to the strain of his long, hard drive from the north country and the worry brought on by the Greebles. With rest and care and good food he'll be all right in a month or so. But it's important that he leave here at once."

The children assisted Traver Nelson with his fur jacket and cap. Then Dr. Jacques threw several blankets around the man and he and Mr. Stamp carried the dog breeder to the snowmobile.

Mr. Stamp started the motor and drove as fast as he could back to the Hollister's cabin.

"Right this way," Mrs. Hollister said. "Put him in our bedroom. We'll take care of him."

"But this will be too much trouble," Traver Nelson objected.

Mrs. Hollister smiled. "I have three little nurses to assist me," she said.

"Me first," Sue offered. "You can wear Daddy's 'jamas, Mr. Nelson. I'll get some."

While the doctor was in the room alone with his patient, Mr. Stamp patted Fluff and remarked, "It's certainly a shame that Traver Nelson can't drive his sled in the race again this year. I'm sure this dog would win it."

"But Mr. Nelson's other Huskies were stolen by

the Greebles," Pam spoke up. "We forgot to tell you that."

She suddenly went to the window and looked out. The brothers' cabin was dark. Evidently the men had not returned and the girl began to wonder if they ever would be caught.

"I could find a couple of Huskies," Mr. Stamp said in a low voice, as if talking to himself. "Fluff could lead any team to victory. If only I could find two more——"

Suddenly Pete stepped forward. "Mr. Stamp," he said, "We could borrow Pierre's dogs. I can manage a komatik. If I learned to drive a team well, could I enter the race?"

"Mr. Stamp, could I enter the race?"

CHAPTER 16

Holly's Secret

AT PETE's suggestion that he drive a team in the dog-sled race, the postman and Mr. Hollister exchanged glances with Gramp.

"By George!" exclaimed Mr. Stamp. "I believe you are clever enough to do it, Pete."

"Indeed he is!" declared Gramp, his eyes twinkling. "Mr. Stamp, you and I could teach this young man the fine points in a hurry."

"Tomorrow's the last day to register," Pete said excitedly.

"I'll fix that," the postman promised. "And I'll get those two Huskies I told you about. Pete, suppose you phone Pierre about his dogs."

Mr. Hollister insisted they get Mr. Nelson's permission first, and this was readily obtained. Then Pete hurried off to Gramp's cabin and put in the call to Pierre. His friend thought the idea a fine one and said he would bring his dogs over before school the next morning. Pete rushed back.

"Everything's set," he reported, "except one thing. We must get Mr. Nelson's komatik. It's at the shack where we found him."

"I'll meet you at the practice place tomorrow."

Mr. Hollister said he would go with Pete directly
after breakfast and drag it to their cabin.

Gramp was almost as excited about the whole
affair as his grandson. "I know a perfect place across
a lake near here where we can practice," he said.

Presently Dr. Jacques came from Mr. Nelson's
room, saying the patient was better already. As he
and Mr. Stamp said good-by, the postman turned in
the doorway.

"I'll meet you at the practice place your grandfather suggested after my mail delivery tomorrow,
Pete. About two o'clock."

When the door closed, Mrs. Hollister hurried to
the kitchen to prepare a late supper. Then the entire
Hollister family, including the grandparents, sat
down to eat.

"What a 'citing 'venture," Sue said as she rubbed her eyes sleepily.

"We'll sure have a lot to tell Miss Nelson when we get home," Ricky remarked.

When everyone had finished supper, Pete hurried to a window and looked at the Greeble brothers' cabin. It still remained in darkness.

"Two Mounties are guarding the place," Gramp said. "And others are out looking for the men. Let's hope they're captured soon."

After the grandparents said good night and left for their cottage, Mrs. Hollister told the children they must retire. Tomorrow would be a full day. Before tumbling into bed, they inquired how Mr. Nelson was getting along. Their mother opened the door and tiptoed in to look at her patient.

"He's asleep now and seems much better," she reported, smiling, when she came back.

It was arranged that Mr. and Mrs. Hollister would take the boys' room, and their sons were to sleep on two spare cots which were set up in the living room.

Next morning, Pete and his father were up early. They hurried off to get Mr. Nelson's special racing komatik. Just as they returned with it, Pierre arrived on snowshoes, holding his two Huskies on leashes.

"Good luck!" he said to Pete as the dogs nuzzled their temporary master.

Pete was impatient for the hour to arrive when he would try out the dog team. Pam reminded him that in the meantime they were to go to Froston and watch the children's ski jumping.

"Ruthie would be disappointed if we don't come." Holly spoke up, giggling and looking at her mother.

The way Mrs. Hollister smiled back at her young daughter made Pam suspect some kind of a secret between them. But nothing more was said. When Gramp arrived with Gallant and the sleigh, all the children but Holly seemed surprised that the entire family was going.

Upon reaching the carnival area, the visitors found it more festive than ever. Flags of various countries were flying on standards and officials were hurrying about. Many onlookers, dressed in gay, colorful clothes, chatted excitedly as they waited for the skiing events.

"Ruthie's class is first," said Holly as she noted

Next came Ruthie.

a young boy take off from the children's jump. He landed perfectly and whizzed off across the slope. Next came Ruthie, looking like a beautiful bird in flight.

"She's amazing," Mr. Hollister declared.

"And she's a good teacher, too," said Holly. "Oh, I hope she wins!"

After all the young ski jumpers had performed, there was a pause of several minutes. Then over the loud-speaker came a man's voice:

"Results of the children's ski jumping: First place to little Ruthie Jansen of Norway."

"Hurrah!" shouted all the Hollister children—all except Holly. She had disappeared.

"Where is Holly?" Pam asked her mother.

"Just listen and keep your eyes open," Mrs. Hollister replied, smiling.

After the announcer had told who had won second and third places, he said, "The next event will be a ski race among children who are beginners in the sport. Nine Canadians and one little girl from the United States have signed up. She's Holly Hollister, granddaughter of the owners of Snowflake Camp."

"Mother!" cried Pam. "You knew it all the time!"

"Yes, and Dad and Gram and Gramp."

Holly's brothers and sisters were so excited they jumped around and waved their arms. As soon as the names of all the contestants had been read, the skiers lined up.

Bang! The starting gun. The children were off!

"Ooh!" cried Sue as a boy nearly bumped Holly.

For a hundred feet the race went well. Then three Canadian girls fell. A moment later two boys ran into each other and down they went! The other five rushed along the slope.

"Yikes!" Ricky yelled as two more local contestants collided and were out of the race. "Holly's still in! Go, Holly!"

His sister wore no hat and her pigtails were standing out straight in the breeze. She and two boys were now whizzing neck and neck toward the finish line.

Suddenly Holly bent still lower on her skis and gave a little bounce. The Hollisters caught their breaths. Had she tripped? No! The movement had given her an extra spurt.

"Holly wins! Holly wins!" Ricky screamed as she crossed the line, and all the Happy Hollisters hugged one another.

They hurried off to congratulate her at the judges' stand and watch the little girl receive a prize. It was a small silver cup, engraved with the event and date.

"That was splendid!" said Mr. Hollister, beaming, and the others joined in.

After watching the other young skiers perform, the Hollisters went home. During lunch, which Gram and Gramp ate with them, they chatted about how quickly and how well Holly had learned to ski.

"It's all because of Ruthie," said Holly. "Please, Gram, may we invite her to Thanksgiving dinner? She never had one."

"This is so 'citing!" said Sue.

"Why certainly, dear," Gram replied. "You run over after lunch and ask her. And how about our including Pierre?"

"Oh yes," all the children cried, and Ricky was chosen to give the invitation.

Pete was secretly hoping that he might come out as well in his contest as Holly and Ruthie had in theirs. But it was a lot to expect and he would be racing against experienced men.

And then there was a possibility the Greebles might show up and cause trouble. So far the two men had not returned and the police had not located them.

Just before two o'clock Gramp drove up in the sleigh and all the children and the three Huskies piled in. What a load there was! Mr. Hollister tied the komatik to the rear and Gallant started off.

"This is so 'citing!" Sue exclaimed.

As they glided along for their meeting with Mr. Stamp, Gramp said, "A dog team can average twenty to thirty miles a day. Commander MacMillan, the famous explorer, drove his team a hundred miles in eighteen hours."

"Yikes!" said Ricky.

"Do Eskimo dogs gallop like horses?" Sue asked.

"Yes. That way they can make twenty miles an hour. But usually they keep to a fast, steady trot."

Presently, Gallant came to the lake shore and trotted out over the ice, which was covered by a light layer of snow. When they reached the far side, Ricky cried:

"I see the snowmobile. There's Mr. Stamp with two Huskies!"

He pointed to a knot of fir trees and Gramp turned Gallant in that direction. As they passed a large hole in the ice, the little boy asked why it was there.

"Somebody has been fishing through the ice," Gramp replied.

"Hi, there!" Mr. Stamp called as they pulled up.

Fluff leaped from the sleigh and ran to the Huskies the postman was holding. The other two in the sleigh jumped out also, and soon the five animals seemed to be holding a conversation.

"They're friends!" Sue exclaimed gleefully.

Pete was relieved. This would make it easier to handle the team.

"First you must learn to harness the five dogs,"

Gramp said, and had Pete help him tie first one dog and then another to the gang hitch. "You see we hook them in pairs to this towline," he explained, "with Fluff running in the lead."

When they were ready, Mr. Stamp reached into the snowmobile and pulled out a long whip. Holly looked at him fearfully.

"Do you spank the dogs with that?" she asked.

Mr. Stamp laughed. "Of course not," he said. "We don't whip the animals. We only crack this to excite the Huskies and make them go faster." He flicked his wrist and cracked the whip a few times, then Pete took a turn.

"Now drive the team," Gramp said. "Slowly."

Pete hopped onto the back of the sled, holding the whip in his right hand.

He slid straight toward the hole!

"*Mush!*" he cried, and the dogs set off.

At once they went at a faster clip than the boy had intended. But by saying "gee" to go right and "haw" to go left, and using the brake as Mr. Stamp directed, Pete guided the team past obstacles in his way. Then the boy took Fluff and the team out onto the surface of the lake. It would be nice and smooth there and easy going for a beginner.

Pete thought he would try the whip. As he cracked it a little, he said, "*Mush, Fluff! Faster!*"

The beautiful dog turned quickly and started to gallop across the surface of the lake. Suddenly the komatik skidded.

Pete was thrown off! Hitting the ice, he slid straight toward the hole the fisherman had made!

CHAPTER 17

A Missing Passenger

"Oh!" screamed Pam as Pete slid toward the hole in the ice.

But just as the boy came to the edge of it, he gave a quick flip and rolled out of the way.

The other children rushed up to him, followed by Gramp and Mr. Stamp.

"Whew!" Gramp said, putting an arm around Pete's shoulder. "That was a close one!"

The postman added, "I guess you learned a good lesson, Pete. You took that turn too fast."

"I'll be more careful," Pete promised.

Fluff had trotted back to him. Once more the boy stepped onto the komatik and drove the dogs around the lake. This time Pete controlled the team much better, and finally he tried racing for a short time.

After an hour of practice, Gramp called to his grandson. "Good work, Pete," he said, his voice full of pride. "You're a natural dog-sled driver."

"It's Fluff," the boy insisted. "She's wonderful."

"That's because she likes you," Pam said. "Fluff knows you helped her master." Pam looked up at her grandfather. "That'll make it easier in the race, won't it?"

"It sure will," Gramp replied. "Fluff is a wise race dog. She'll keep the rest of the team in line for you, Pete. And now, I think we should go over to the course and drive around it several times."

Mr. Stamp offered to take the other children to the cabin in the snowmobile. When Ricky reached home, he rushed up to his parents, who met them at the door, and shouted:

"Yikes! Pete can drive a dog team as well as an Eskimo can."

Mr. and Mrs. Hollister smiled. "Do you think Pete has just a little chance of winning?" his mother asked.

"A little chance!" Mr. Stamp exclaimed. "I'd say he has a fine chance if everything is fair and square and not like last year."

After he had driven off, Mr. Hollister looked at his wife and winked.

"Shall we tell them now?" he asked.

Mrs. Hollister smiled. "I think we should, John."

"What's the big secret?" Pam asked.

"We've just received a telegram from Miss Nelson," her father said. "She'll arrive in Froston tomorrow morning on the ten o'clock train."

"Goodie!" Holly exclaimed. "Then she can eat turkey with us."

"And here's more good news," said Mr. Hollister. "Dr. Jacques visited Traver Nelson this afternoon and said he could eat Thanksgiving dinner with us."

They all sang Thanksgiving hymns.

Pam clapped her hands happily. "Oh, what a wonderful time we'll have!"

That evening Traver Nelson gave Pete some instructions about the race course.

"If you think you can pass the team ahead of you," he said, "be sure not to come too close to it. Give the other driver plenty of room. Otherwise the dogs' harnesses may become tangled. And that narrow ravine halfway along the track—don't try to pass anyone in there."

It was decided that Pete would have another practice period early Thanksgiving morning. He and his brother and sisters were up early and Sue ran around excitedly calling out:

"Happy Thanksgiving, everybody!"

Following a custom which Gram and Gramp had

always kept, the whole family gathered in the living room around the roaring fire and sang Thanksgiving hymns. Then each member told what he had been particularly thankful for during the past year. At the end Gram said:

"And one of our great blessings is that we still are the *Happy* Hollisters."

After breakfast Gramp and Pete went out with the dogs. Mr. Hollister hitched up Gallant and set off with the other children to meet Miss Nelson. Several minutes before reaching the station they could see the train slowly pulling out. It had discharged the Froston passengers and was on its way again.

"Oh, we're late!" Pam exclaimed. "I hope Miss Nelson won't be upset."

When Gallant stopped at the wooden platform, the children saw several men being greeted by friends. But Miss Nelson was not in sight.

"Maybe she's inside or has walked around the station looking for us," Pam said a trifle nervously.

Their teacher was not inside the station nor on the other side of it.

"Do you suppose she missed the train at Shoreham?" Holly asked.

"Oh no," Pam said, still glancing about. "Miss Nelson would have let us know." Secretly she was worried that the Greeble brothers might have interfered with the teacher's trip. "I'll ask the stationmaster if he saw her."

The stationmaster was busy checking baggage.

"Did you see a tall, nice-looking woman get off the train?" Pam asked him.

The man looked up. "Why, yes I did," he said. "But she hurried off immediately."

"Where?"

"Through that door into the baggage room," the stationmaster replied.

Pam thanked him and said to the others, "I'll look there." She hastened to the baggage room, stacked high with suitcases, sacks of mail, and big cartons.

"Miss Nelson! Miss Nelson!" Pam called.

There was silence for a moment. Then the girl heard a whispered reply. "Is that you, Pam?"

The teacher stepped from behind a high pile of boxes and looked worriedly out the door.

"You've been hiding!" Pam said as she rushed over to give Miss Nelson a hug.

The teacher explained that just as she had stepped off the train she had seen Mr. Stockman and Mr. Gates. Wishing to avoid them, Miss Nelson had hurried into the waiting room.

"When they came in there, I dashed into the baggage room," she said.

Pam was amazed to hear that the two men were near by. She told Miss Nelson about the bearded campers and how she suspected they were really Stockman and Gates.

"Taking off their beards would be kind of a disguise up here," Pam said excitedly. "The police wouldn't be looking for them without beards."

"They found my brother!" the teacher cried.

Quickly the girl went outside and told an officer what she thought. Together they hunted for Stockman and Gates around the station but could not find the men. Finally they gave up, but the policeman said he would report the incident.

In the meantime the other children and their father had greeted Miss Nelson. Pam joined them and they drove to Snowflake Camp.

"To think you found my brother!" the teacher kept saying over and over. "This is the most wonderful Thanksgiving I've ever had!"

When they reached the cabin, she went at once to see Traver Nelson. What a joyful meeting it was!

The Hollisters left the room so the twin brother and sister could be alone for a little while. At one o'clock Ruthie and Pierre arrived. After they were introduced to Miss Nelson, the whole group set off for Gram and Gramp's cottage.

The older Hollisters welcomed Miss Nelson and their other guests and Gram added, "Dinner is ready. Come, find your places."

Pam had made cards with the names on. When everyone was seated, Gramp carried in the turkey and placed it on the table.

"What a big gobbler!" Ricky shrieked in delight, and Gram said it weighed thirty pounds.

Gramp, standing at the head of the table, sharpened the carving knife. When he finished, he said, "I think it would be nice for my grandchildren to say Grace together today."

When all heads were bowed, the group from Shoreham said a little Thanksgiving prayer. Then, as the conversation started again, Pam looked at everyone with a twinkle in her eye. Reaching under her plate, she held up seven slips of paper in one fist. She explained that each child who wanted a leg of the turkey should draw a slip.

"The two shortest are for the drumsticks," she said, holding the slips toward Ruthie.

How the children giggled as each pulled out a strip!

"Ricky and Pierre get the drumsticks," Pam said.

"Then may I have the wishbone?" Holly pleaded. "I have an awfully important wish to make with it."

Gramp carved it out and the wishbone was handed to the little girl. She took it to the kitchen to dry.

It was a wonderful dinner, with cranberry sauce, onions, mashed potatoes, candied sweet potatoes, celery and olives, and tall glasses of milk. As everyone concentrated on eating, Gram looked up and chuckled.

"How strangely silent it has become! Be sure to leave room for dessert!" she warned.

When everyone had finished the main course, she got up from the table and beckoned Pete to accompany her to the kitchen. After Pam and Holly had cleared the table, the boy and his grandmother returned with two large pies. Gram held an apple pie and Pete a pumpkin pie with whipped cream on top.

When Traver Nelson saw them, his eyes glistened. "All this is better than medicine for me," he declared. "You Hollisters have made me get well in a hurry."

After dinner everyone sat in front of the fireplace and nibbled on nuts and mints.

Holly's wish was for Pete to win the race.

"Oh!" Pete groaned. "I hope I'm still not so stuffed tomorrow I can't drive in the race."

"I'd say you'd have more strength than ever," Miss Nelson said cheerily.

Just then Holly exclaimed, "Gram, is the wishbone dry enough to wish on yet?"

"I think it is," Gram replied, and hustled into the kitchen to bring Holly her prize.

"I want Mother to wish with me," the girl said.

Holly held one end of the bone and her mother the other. Then Holly looked up at the ceiling and tickled her nose with her pigtail while she thought about her wish.

"Ready?" her mother asked.

"Yes."

They both pulled and Holly wished that Pete would win the next day. *Snap!* Mrs. Hollister's part broke off and Holly won!

During the evening the group had fun singing and playing games.

"This is the bestest Thanksgiving ever," Sue told her grandmother as they left for home.

"It's a wonderful custom," Ruthie declared. "I wish my country would adopt it."

As the Hollisters started back toward their cabin, it began to snow.

"Just what we need for a good race course," Pete said happily. "I hope it's dry so Fluff won't have to race in boots."

Next morning at ten o'clock hundreds of people

lined the course for the dog-sled race. Three teams were at the starting line and suddenly another appeared.

"Why, it's a young boy!" one of the spectators gasped.

"And he's driving Fluff!" said another. "It's a surprise entry!"

The veterinarian checked Fluff and her teammates. They passed without a question and Pete went to the starting line. Mr. Rice, the chairman, announced that Pete was racing in place of Traver Nelson, who had been ill. A shout went up from the crowd.

"Ready!"

The starting gun went off and the race began!

Bang! The race began.

179

CHAPTER 18

The Big Race

THE three men in the dog-sled race with Pete had so much more experience driving Huskies that they quickly got ahead of the boy.

"Oh, Pete is trailing!" Holly wailed.

"Don't worry," Mrs. Hollister calmed her. "It's a long race course and Pete still has a chance."

Pete, meanwhile, cracked his whip in the air and urged his team along. "*Mush! Mush!*" he shouted, and could feel a stronger pull from his dogs.

As he rounded the first bend in the course, he remembered his experience on the lake, and used his brake to advantage. Soon he began to gain on the teams ahead of him. As he drew abreast of the last one, Pete shouted once more:

"*Mush, Fluff! Mush!*"

The great dog's muscles strained as she pulled harder and harder, urging the other Huskies along with her. Pete's komatik edged past the man in front of him. Now he was third!

By this time the onlookers were shouting wildly and the Hollisters were screaming Fluff's name. The dog seemed to know exactly when to take a spurt and galloped past the second-place team. Pete gave it plenty of room as Traver Nelson had instructed him.

"If I can only catch that first team!" Pete thought.

But the dogs in the lead were very fast. Pete gained on them for a while, then dropped back.

"Fluff!" Pete shouted, and cracked the whip again.

The faithful animal surged forward with a tremendous burst of speed. For a few yards Fluff raced neck and neck with the opposing king dog. Then she pulled steadily into the lead. Pete passed his last opponent!

"Oh, nothing must stop me now!" the boy thought excitedly. "I must drive well."

Not far from the finish line Pete saw something which made his spine tingle with fear. Stockman and Gates, standing at the top of a little hill, rolled a log toward the path of the speeding dog team! If it hit them, everything would be lost!

Using his brake, he screamed, "Fluff! Danger! Gee!"

Fluff seemed to understand. She swerved to the right, avoiding the rolling log by inches. The lurch nearly threw Pete off balance, but he clung to the komatik as Fluff turned back on the course and made a beeline for the finish tape.

"Pete's going to win!" Ricky cried excitedly.

Pam had been standing with Holly and Ricky some distance from her parents and the Nelsons and seen the rolling log. As Pete's sled flashed across the finish line, she and the others ran to find Mr. Stamp. They quickly told him what had happened.

Ricky tugged at their beards.

"I saw the men run toward that lake," Pam said, pointing.

"We'll chase them!" the postman said angrily.

The three climbed into his snowmobile and it roared off.

"There they are, right in the middle of the ice!" Ricky shouted.

When the two men heard the snowmobile, they glanced over their shoulders. Both wore beards.

"Why, they're the Greeble brothers!" Mr. Stamp said, puzzled.

"I'm sure they're just disguised," Pam insisted.

Mr. Stamp chased them in circles until the men fell to the snow, exhausted. Then he stopped the snowmobile.

Ricky was the first to jump off. He ran to the two men and tugged at their beards. Off they came!

"We've caught you!" Ricky shouted.

The postman quickly reached into his snowmobile and pulled out two leather straps which he used to bundle his mail. As the children watched in awe, Mr. Stamp tied their wrists behind their backs.

"Now get up," he ordered, "and climb into the car."

As they drove back, Pam asked their prisoners one question after another. Yes, the men said, they had wanted Fluff because she was probably the world's best Eskimo dog. They had not been able to find her and thought Traver Nelson might return to Froston and race again this year. That was why they had come there.

"We didn't know Snowflake Camp belonged to your grandparents," Mr. Gates growled, "or that you Hollister kids would upset all our plans."

As the snowmobile reached the shore, a policeman hurried to meet them.

"Oh, Mr. Mountie!" Holly shouted. "We have two bad men for you!"

As the Mountie snapped handcuffs on the pair, he praised their captors. Then he said, "You men are the ones who hurt Fluff in the race last year!"

Ricky gazed straight at them. "But you didn't get away with it this year. And Pete won!"

At this very moment, Pete was about to receive a silver cup. His brother and sisters hurried back, reaching him just as the boy accepted it. The captain of the Mounties turned to Traver Nelson.

"We'll buy all of Fluff's puppies if you want to sell them," he said.

"I'd like to," replied Mr. Nelson. Then he gripped Pete's hand. "I can never thank you enough," he said. "You've made this the happiest day of my life!"

"And for me, too," added Miss Nelson.

Suddenly Gramp exclaimed, "Goodness! Here comes more excitement!"

They turned to see a truck being driven toward them. On the back of it was a big motion picture camera.

"Look up here, Pete, and the rest of your family!" the operator said, and the camera whirred away.

"Why are you taking pictures of us Happy Hollisters and Fluff?" Sue asked.

"These movies are for television," the man replied. "We took pictures of the race. And now for the close-ups."

The children laughed and waved at the camera.

"That's fine!" the cameraman shouted. "Now people all over the United States and Canada will have a chance to see the Happy Hollisters on their television sets!"